LOVE BY MOONLIGHT
SOLHAVEN FOREVERS
BOOK TWO

LIZ MARTINSON

This is a work of fiction. Names, characters, places, and incidents are products of the author's imagination or are used fictitiously and are not to be construed as real. Any resemblance to actual events, locales, organizations or persons, living or dead, is entirely coincidental.

Love By Moonlight, Copyright © 2023 Liz Martinson

All rights reserved. No part of this book may be reproduced in any form or by any electronic or mechanical means, including information storage and retrieval systems, without written permission from the author, except for the use of brief quotations in a book review.

WARNING DISCLAIMER: This collection is suited for Adults 18+ only. Stories contain sexual situations and adult language. All characters depicted are of legal age.

Book Cover Design ©The Cover Fling

INTRODUCTION

There's something about Solhaven—Solhaven and love seem to go hand in hand, so beware if you visit.

Laid-back Jake has sworn off commitment, but falls for business woman Emily. Sweet Claire wins over Daniel, who arrives full of despair. Lizzie lacks confidence and is helped through her angst by the mysterious gardener, Anton.

Perhaps it's the sea air? Maybe there's a kelpie keeping watch who likes to lend a helping hand?

Whatever it is, true love is found in the tranquil and beautiful coastal scenery of south Wales, with its secret coves and peaceful beaches.

You'll fall in love with Solhaven itself, and which couple will prove to be your favourite?

The series Solhaven Forevers is set in a small town in Wales, UK.

The books are written in British English.

CHAPTER 1

Claire Bradstock twirled around in the small cottage at the bottom of the Haven House Hotel grounds, set on the very edge of the glorious sweep of Haven Bay. Delighted she was back in her beloved Wales, her heart sang. She'd made it! Changed careers to something she'd always loved doing, and which she knew would be way less stressful than teaching. It had taken determination, tenacity and hard work, and she'd been left with almost no free time at all over the last three years, but oh, it had been worth it.

She'd loved being a teacher, but as the years had passed, the record keeping and goal-setting had taken all the joy away, and she'd ended up feeling as if she was letting the kids down. Hating the dissatisfaction, knowing there was nothing she could do to change the system, she'd thought long and hard about her future and finally decided to do something entirely different.

Always a lover of the outdoors, and the person who'd tended their garden at home while her dad had been ill, Claire was determined to train as a gardener. Being her own boss and seeing what was in her charge flourish for a change. Creating beauty. Growing food. She was that sort—caring, nourishing, kind. She was always the one who would buy a homeless person a coffee and some food, or stop to help if she thought someone was in need.

She'd enrolled at a local university to complete her degree in horticulture, and spent every holiday, in all kinds of weather, gaining practical experience. She'd worked in gardens and market gardens, and sometimes on arable farms, learning about crops. None of it had been easy, but she was proud of what she'd achieved, and she loved everything she'd learned.

Then the icing on the cake. Claire hugged herself, now grinning in glee as she remembered the phone call. Late last November, with only the rest of the school year between her and becoming unemployed, her mum had called.

'Claire, cariad. You won't believe this! You really won't—'

'Hi, mum. Yes, thanks, I'm very well. Things are pretty quiet here at the moment. How are you?'

'Oh, sorry, I do run on, don't I? Yes, yes... how are you then? Oh, but you just told me, didn't you? Listen... you're never going to believe this!'

Curious, Claire had settled onto the settee in her small flat, smiling at her mother's excited voice. 'Okay, so what won't I believe?'

'Well, see, it's hard to know where to start. You

know old Mr Whitchurch, who took Jake under his wing?'

'Duh, yes, mum.' Claire's smile had broadened. Mr Whitchurch had been a kind, elderly man with no son of his own and a penchant for surfing, so had sponsored Jake when her brother was competing.

'He's left the estate, Claire, the estate, mind you, to Jake. The house and the café, with the access road and car park. Jake didn't want me to tell you until they executed the will, or something.'

Eyebrows lifting, Claire had felt pleased for her little brother, whose career had been cut short three years ago by an accident which had caused spinal damage. 'That's great! I know Mr Whitchurch had promised him the café, but the house as well? My, my, he'll be too posh for us now.'

Her mum had laughed. 'Well, wait until you hear this! He's given the house away.'

'He's what?'

'Given it away.'

'You're joking. You have to be. He wouldn't be so daft.'

For despite Jake's tendency to drift through his life apparently doing nothing much, Claire knew how hard he'd worked to achieve his position in the surfing world before his accident. She was aware he did a damn good job with the café, too, and it wasn't just holiday makers who went there, but locals as well. And at old Mr Whitchurch's insistence, he also had a decent property portfolio. His sponsor had always told him never to fritter his money away, but to make it work for him, so to give Haven House away seemed inconceivable.

'No, I'm not joking. He's given it away, but he's going to live there, as well. Oh, Claire, Jake's finally settled down. He really has. With Emily. Have I said anything about her? Probably not, because at first, I thought she was just one of his candy-flosses, but it turns out they really love each other. And she's so different from his other ones. She's older, for a start, and a businesswoman. Opposite of Jake in lots of ways.'

Claire had sunk back on the settee, her eyes wide. 'I can't believe it. You're pulling my leg. I thought I'd settle down before Jake. Are you sure it's solid?'

'Completely. She's going to turn the house into a hotel, and they'll live in the attics. But this is where you come in, see? Emily needs a gardener, and I thought you might be interested because I know you want to come home. She wants to interview you at Christmas, when you come here for the holidays. She's going to restore all the grounds back to what it was like when the house was built, apparently, so it'll be a big job, mind.'

The interview had gone well, and Emily and Claire had formed an instant bond. The hotel had opened nearly four months ago, back at Easter, and until Claire could start work, Emily had employed some contractors to keep the place tidy.

And here she was, officially a gardener and in the delighted occupation of a cottage she'd loved all her life. As Mr Whitchurch had occasionally used the cottage for guests, it came with a double bed, a cooker, and some basic furniture, so she'd chosen to store her furniture until she'd had some time to adjust to her surroundings, outside and in.

Not only officially a gardener, but in sole charge of starting the restoration of the Victorian grounds, and the kitchen gardens, as they'd been when the house was built. The challenge, getting to work, excited her, though apprehension pricked at her as well. It was an enormous task, but Emily apparently had the original plans, which would help a lot, and at her interview, she'd reassured Claire this would be an extensive project covering several years before completion. It was so incredibly exciting to have landed a job like this. She would do her best.

Her mobile pinged, breaking into her reminiscences and the pleasure at being home.

It was a text from Jake asking her, of all things, if she could work in the restaurant tonight. Apparently, a couple of their staff had phoned in sick, so they were short, and, he pointed out, he knew she could wait on because she'd had holiday jobs in the café.

A far cry from dreaming about her gardens, spending the evening waiting on! Laughing, remembering those times when Jake had sent the same plea, but to come help out at his café, Claire texted back an affirmative before shooting upstairs for a shower. Not quite what she'd envisaged for her first night, but it would be a bit of fun. The sunset and bottle of wine could wait until tomorrow.

Drying herself, she pulled on a navy cotton skirt and white shirt and dragged a brush through her thick, dark-blonde hair, which fell in heavy waves around her shoulders, before tying it back into a low ponytail.

Picking up her bag, she let herself out just as Jake drove down the narrow track at the side of the hotel grounds. The distance between the cottage and hotel was slightly more than a quarter of a mile, normally easily walkable, but tonight, Jake had played nice and come to collect her in one of the two small buggies they kept up at the hotel.

'Hiya, little brother.' She smiled at him as she climbed in. 'Thanks for the lift.'

'Claire.' He shot her a grin. 'Settled in? Like the cottage?'

'Like it? How could I not? It's amazing. But I still worry that you and Emily could have used it as guest accommodation?'

'Nah. We talked about it, but it's too far away from the hotel. We don't want cars down here, and we didn't want to lend out any of the buggies regularly. Anyway, it's called Gardener's Cottage, so yours by default.'

'Yes, but rent-free? On top of a decent wage, as well.'

'I know you'll earn it. Probably do loads of overtime into the bargain.'

'Is Mum enjoying working here too?'

Jake pulled the buggy round the corner of the beautiful Victorian house and stopped by the back door. 'Loving it. And she's damned good at it.'

'Why isn't Emily waiting on tonight? Not that I mind doing it at all, but I just thought she'd be the first to step in.'

He rested his arm on the wheel and turned towards her. 'She's tired.'

'Doesn't sound like Emily. I hope she's okay?' She looked questioningly at her brother, but instead of him looking worried, a sheepish, yet delighted grin was breaking out on his face.

'No!' Emily exclaimed. 'How far on is she?'

'Coming up to four months, and she says it may as well become general knowledge because she's beginning to show—just.' He glowed with pride.

'Oh, Jake!' Claire's eyes filled with happy tears as she looked at her easy-going, handsome, surfing brother. She'd always thought he would never settle down, never have a meaningful relationship. 'I'm so pleased for you both. But…' she hesitated a moment before diving in. 'Are *you* happy about this? Really happy?'

Jake's face was serious as he looked at his sister. 'Couldn't be happier. You don't know what Emily's done for me, and how much I love her.'

'I'm pleased for you both,' Claire repeated, as she grinned and punched him lightly on the arm. 'And I don't mind waiting on. Any evening, if you're short.'

'Ah, we don't expect to be busy tonight, and I'll be around as well. Jenny's closing the cafe for me today.'

Claire got out of the buggy and entered the hotel, finding her way to the lounge, thinking wistfully of her own lack of love life. Her previous boyfriend had given up on her half-way through her studies. He'd thought the whole idea of becoming a gardener was a step down in the world, despite her protests and mentioning various well-known television gardeners. He'd replied scathingly they were all men, implying women were useless at the job. If he hadn't walked, she would have pushed. His lack of faith in women and his contempt for her change of career had been the writing on the wall. Ah, well… she was confident it would happen someday.

'Hey, Claire.' Emily stood behind the small drinks bar in a corner of the lounge, wiping the already gleaming woodwork with a pristine cloth. 'Settling in okay?'

'Great. I love that cottage and Jake's just reassured me for the millionth time why you didn't want it as guest accommodation. Oh, and he let something out, too. Congratulations!' She leaned forwards to kiss Emily's cheek then slid onto a stool, resting her forearms on the spotless counter.

Emily smiled, her hand resting on the slight bump which, now Claire looked carefully, she could just see. 'Thanks. We're thrilled about it. And look, we're not being kind or anything about the cottage. Just glad you don't mind being isolated.'

'Oh, come on, hardly isolated. I can see the hotel, and it's only about a mile along the sands to Solhaven.'

'The sands, yes. About two miles on the cliff path, and that's mostly up and down!'

The cliff path along the whole of the coast was hard work, but the stunning scenery would reward anyone prepared to walk it. Emily and Jake had employed Dominic Winchester, a friend of Emily's brother, to design the conversion of the old garage and outhouses into three cottages and some hostel accommodation for walkers. To attract the walkers, they'd put a sign just below Gardener's Cottage, directing them up to the hotel, as well as running adverts on numerous tourist sites. It was a good move. Much of the visitor accommodation in Solhaven wasn't for a casual night or two, so they were filling a sizeable gap in the market. As well as the holiday accommodation, the architect had also designed the conversion of the attics of the hotel into an amazing living space for Emily and Jake.

'I still can't believe how Jake's changed,' Claire murmured.

Amused, Emily raised her brows. 'How changed?'

'Oh, just *happier*. It's obvious he adores you—'

'It's mutual.'

'And now the baby's coming, and he's immensely thrilled about that, I could tell.'

'Ha! I think he's hoping for a surfer dude baby.'

They laughed.

'Maybe I can see the change more because I've been away.'

'Maybe.' Emily gave a half-smile and shrugged. 'Oh, yes… Jake's been telling me you paint seascapes and local beauty spots for a hobby? I hope you'll find some time to continue?'

'I haven't painted anything since I was here at Easter. Geoff down at the Shell Gallery takes a few from me to sell, and he's turned a couple into cards.'

'Impressive! I think it's great that you sell some. I wouldn't know where to start.'

Claire gave a self-deprecating smile. 'I'm an amateur.'

'We all have to start somewhere.' Emily grinned. 'Do some of the hotel and round about the grounds, and we can sell them in here, maybe?'

'Would you?' Claire's face lit up. 'That's kind of you. Helps towards buying new paints.'

Through the open door, they saw some people pass through the hall, on their way to the dining-room.

'Looks like things are warming up.' Emily nodded towards a disappearing couple.

'I better shift myself.' Claire slid off her stool and grinned. 'You realise I'm only Jake's Café trained? No silver service here.'

'You'll be fine. It's been a fairly slow start to the tourist season this year, but it'll get busier now it's the summer holidays. And thanks for helping us out. This isn't exactly in your job description!'

Laughing, Claire flipped a wave as she disappeared. It would be amusing serving again, and anyway, there might be someone she knew who'd come for a meal, and they could have a catch-up.

Nearly four hours later, Claire surreptitiously eased her shoulders and flexed her feet, regarding the almost full restaurant with a wry smile. Mmm, not so much amusing as damned hard work! So Jake had said it would be quiet mid-week, and Emily had claimed it would be slow? Huh! They'd been rushed off their feet for the first part of the evening, and it was only recently things had quietened. Most people had reached the dessert or coffee stage, and there had only been two or three additional groups who'd come in during the last half hour. Jean, who should have finished at nine, had only just gone home, and Claire had been grateful for her help. She glanced at her watch. Twenty to ten. Surely no one would come in to eat now. The restaurant closed for service at ten.

There was the murmur of conversation, the muted sound of cutlery on china plates and the delicate smell of good food. The lighting was subdued, and the atmosphere relaxed. Emily had done a great job of re-creating a Victorian dining-room with her choice of furniture and decoration. The hotel was small but was apparently doing very well and gaining an excellent reputation. Claire was pleased it was succeeding.

She cleared a table recently vacated by a family of four who'd told her they were down for the weekend, staying in their caravan on the local site above Silver Sands. Quickly and neatly, she re-laid the table, brought coffee to another party at the far side of the room, and served dessert to a couple she had learned were celebrating their engagement. Once more, with a moment of leisure, Claire stood to survey the room, a feeling of satisfaction stealing over her at a job well done. Bit different to teaching biology!

'Does it matter where I sit?' The voice behind her was deep, and shot through with weariness. It pierced Claire, sending a shiver down her back.

Turning slowly, her eyes met those of the man standing in the doorway. For no obvious reason, her stomach lurched, and she drew in a quick breath, feeling almost boneless.

He was tall and lean, and his face was etched with the lines of sadness and suffering. Despite his obvious emotional pain, he stood with authority, hands thrust into the pockets of creased, faded denims which clung to the length of his lean thighs. A fine, white cotton shirt, hanging loose round narrow hips, emphasised the breadth of his shoulders, and the rolled-back sleeves displayed muscled forearms. Claire brought her eyes back up to his face. Not conventionally good-looking. His jaw was square and uncompromising, his gaze coolly grey and rock-steady on her. He looked exhausted as well as upset, with shadows under his thickly lashed eyes, and his mouth showed no trace of a smile. Dark brown hair curled onto the collar of his shirt, unruly and overlong.

For what seemed an eternity she continued to gaze at him, snared by her rush of emotions—she was melting and trembling, and her heart was racing—all because she was looking at a total stranger who offered in return no smile, no sign of interest. No understanding of the effect he was having on her. This was ridiculous. She had to get a grip on herself. But as well as this visceral reaction, her heart ached for his misery. She wanted to reach out and help him, make everything right in his world.

It was the man who broke the thrall that held Claire immobile. He gave a small shake of his head, stepping back as if distancing himself from her. 'I asked if it matters where I sit?'

'No, no... you can sit anywhere,' she finally said.

She was thirty-one, for heaven's sake. No green girl behaving as if she had a crush on the latest hero of the hour. She'd had plenty of boyfriends, a couple of whom had been quite serious relationships. Yet none had made her react like this, and she was only *looking* at the man.

She watched as he strode into the room, glanced round, and chose a table near the wall.

He dominated the room, Claire decided, as she picked up the menu and wine-list to follow him, threading her way between the tables. Such was his presence, she noticed women of other parties covertly eyeing him as he pulled out a chair and sat. He was that sort of man—someone you turned to look at, in a room, on the street. Magnetic? Sexy? Claire couldn't quite define what it was, but he seemed unaware of the attention he attracted.

'I'll have a Tallaig, please.'

Claire handed him the menu and wine list, murmuring something incoherent before fleeing to the safety of the lounge.

'Whoa!' Claire leaned a hand on the bar and rolled her eyes.

Emily looked up from her laptop, a frown creasing her brow. 'What's the matter? You look a bit shaken. There's no trouble, is there? No-one's been rude to you?'

Claire's hands trembled, and she clasped them tightly together. 'No, no trouble. I need a whisky, please. A Tallaig, he said.' Dazed, she replayed her first sight of him and minutely examined her immediate response, but no matter how many times she did this, the result was the same. He'd made an enormous impact on her, and she wanted to know him better. *A lot better*. As a person. And, she admitted to herself in stark honesty, with heat pooling inside, to know him in the biblical sense, too.

'Surely.' Emily served the drink, still looking concerned. 'But if there's no trouble, then what *is* the matter? Because something spooked you, that's obvious.'

'It's weird, but I think I just fell in love,' Claire murmured, disbelief clear in her voice.

'Fell in love?' Emily laughed. 'What do you mean? Impossible!' She eyed Claire with curiosity.

'Didn't you see him?' Claire shook her head in disbelief that anyone might have missed him. 'That man who came through to the dining-room about five minutes ago?'

'Tall chap? Dark hair?'

Claire nodded. 'Him.'

'He was okay, I suppose.' Emily shrugged, looking mystified. 'Come on, Claire. You can't just fall in love with a total stranger! In lust, maybe. But you'd need to get to know him and…' her voice faded.

Watching Emily, Claire knew she was thinking about what had happened between her and Jake. They'd taken one look at each other, according to her mum, and made an instant connection. A connection so strong Emily had changed her entire life for him. 'Like you and Jake, yes?'

Emily threw up her hands. 'Touché!'

'And if it happened to you, it could happen again?'

'I suppose.' Hesitation seemed to lengthen the wait for Emily's reply into an eternity. 'Anyway, you better take him his drink.' She pushed the tumbler of Tallaig towards Claire.

Picking up the glass, Claire returned to the dining-room. Considering herself to be moderately level-headed, Claire found the emotions sweeping through her disconcerting. Anyway, he could be passing through, and after tonight, she would never see him again. Or he might have come just for a holiday, so maybe all she would get was a holiday romance? Ah, but what was the prognosis for one of those? Jake had known the formula off by heart, and both she and her mother had despaired of him. It wasn't what she wanted. One day, she hoped for permanent, but until tonight, she'd never met someone who put the thought of permanent so firmly into her head.

It was ridiculous. *She* was ridiculous.

She paused in the dining-room doorway, her eyes seeking him out, before taking a deep breath, walking over to his table, and placing the whisky next to the long-fingered hand lying loosely on the starched white cloth.

'Are you ready to order now?' she asked.

The stranger looked up and eyed her blankly. 'Eh? Oh, ordering. Yes. I'll have the mixed seafood platter. And I'd like half a bottle of Australian Chardonnay as well, please.' He looked away, blocking any attempts to chat.

'It'll be about twenty minutes.' Claire left, and after dropping the order into the kitchen, went to collect the Chardonnay.

'How're things?' Emily asked cheerfully.

'He's not very forthcoming. Can I have half a bottle of the Chardonnay, please?'

Claire knew herself to be attractive and friendly, and she usually had no difficulties in getting people to open up, but she hadn't had a chance to try with this guy. At a guess, his defences had been up before he'd entered the dining-room. Mind you, he looked rough. Really rough. Whatever was going on inside his head was probably not conducive to socialising with anyone.

Handing her the bottle, Emily looked sympathetic. 'Good luck.'

For Emily, it'd been easy. When they'd first met, Jake had been just as interested as she was.

Without allowing herself pause for thought, Claire walked over to his table, uncorked the wine, and poured some into his glass.

'That's fine,' he said, having perfunctorily tasted it without lifting his eyes from an eBook he was reading.

Within fifteen minutes, she returned with his meal. 'I hope you enjoy it. It's one of the chef's best dishes.'

'Thank you.' He still didn't look at her.

It was as if he'd shut himself off from the world. Perhaps he was trying to come to terms with some terrible trauma. A bereavement, or a dangerous illness he was only now recovering from? Never mind her visceral attraction, her heart went out to him in sympathy.

Moving round the dining room, clearing tables, chatting to the remaining clientele, Claire was aware of his near-motionless figure picking at the meal in front of him. He used his fork and propped his head on his other hand. She wanted so much to offer some sort of help, but he'd likely not appreciate it. She was also trying to rationalise her sudden attraction. Okay, he was good looking, and he seemed very sad and tired, but it couldn't just be that. There had to be more. Something at a much deeper level had sparked between them the moment they'd looked at each other. That seemed to be the real reason, but why had it happened? Something else was bothering her, too. She thought he looked slightly familiar, but for the life of her, she couldn't think where she might have come across him.

When he'd finished the meal, she went back to clear his plate. 'I hope everything was okay?'

'Thank you, yes. It was good. I won't have anything else, but perhaps you can help me?' His voice softened slightly as the corner of his mouth lifted in a half-hearted smile. The soft light from the discreet table lamps brought some warmth to the grey depths of his eyes and a coppery glint to his thick, unruly hair.

'Perhaps,' she acknowledged cautiously, hoping against hope she would be able to.

'I'm looking for some people,' he said. 'A family called Bradstock, and I—'

'Bradstock?' Claire asked, holding onto the back of a chair, unable to believe her ears. Her body went numb again, but from shock this time.

He wanted *her family*?

She still hadn't worked out why he looked familiar, and she'd no idea who he was.

CHAPTER 2

DANIEL MORGAN WAS DESPERATELY tired after the appalling start to yesterday, when he'd come home from his agent's office to find his ex-wife had taken up residence in his house. His very pregnant ex-wife, together with her lover. It didn't help to know it was completely down to his own stupidity. He'd never changed the locks, and he hadn't realised Gina had slipped off with a key. That she'd moved in was unbelievable in view of the fact she'd been the one to walk out on him last year. There was also the other thing she'd done when she—but there, his thoughts stopped. The pain was too much to bear just now. He'd felt exhausted ever since the bereavement and divorce, and had spent the last year recovering. He didn't need her reviving all those bitter memories which he was finally putting behind him.

Like an ancient oil-painting, he felt on the verge of disintegration. Finding Gina had taken up residence in his house had threatened his very sanity. He'd made an instant decision to walk out, and put the whole matter into the hands of his solicitor. In the process, he'd made himself homeless, and had lost access to all his work, which, thank goodness, was safely locked away from Gina's avaricious little paws in his loft studio. Trouble was, there were paintings in the studio which he needed. They were supposed to be with his agent before he left for America in two months' time. Now he needed the coastline so he could paint some replacements.

It was his good friend and mentor, portrait painter Sebastian Whitchurch, who'd offered a viable solution. Sebastian's second or third cousin—he couldn't remember which, only that the man was now dead—had owned a house and a cottage in Solhaven, and had once told Sebastian he would leave them to a young man called Bradstock. Assuming the family now lived in the house, Sebastian had suggested the cottage might be available to rent. An excellent retreat, and one where he could paint as many seascapes as he needed. The sound of it suited Daniel, so today he'd driven a very long way west, to the beautiful coastline of Wales.

Now he was at a hotel called Haven House, looking at a slim woman with a tumbled mass of dark blonde waves falling down her back and large golden-brown eyes.

In view of all that had happened to him in the last couple of years, and the vow he'd taken never to let a woman close again, he found himself disturbed by the unexpected feelings seeping, faint but definite, through him now. Feelings of an instant recognition and a physical response, both of which held him immobile for a few brief, fascinated seconds. Maybe it was a relief to know he could still feel, but loving anyone was no longer on his agenda. Love equated to being hurt, and it wasn't worth it.

Yet her face was gentle and her eyes, so clear and penetrating, seemed able to see his innermost misery, and there was something soothing about her. What would it be like to let go, give in, turn to her for comfort? Then, even more unexpected than those thoughts, and totally unwelcome, he noticed his body's response, a stirring of interest which he immediately stepped back from.

It was only a result of his tiredness and hunger that his defences were down. A desperate justification as he strode off to choose a table. Daniel had no interest in women unless they were the kind who could take a night together and part company the next day with only a casual word of thanks, and he didn't think this one would be that sort. Hopefully, a shot of spirits and some food might boost him sufficiently to find these people he'd been directed to. Then, all he wanted to do was sleep.

Once he'd eaten, he wouldn't have to see the woman again, anyway. He'd find the Bradstocks and hopefully be able to rent this cottage of theirs, then he could avoid the hotel for the rest of the time he'd be here. If he could stay. He was rather dubious about Sebastian's blithe reassurances that it would all be okay, that these people would have somewhere he could stay. His friend had been very vague. His visit to Henry Whitchurch had been many years ago, but he'd recalled the cottage was on the edge of the sea.

Oh, this was all such a fucking *mess*. He was emotionally and physically at the end of his tether. One more setback, and he might just lay his head down on the table and weep.

The sweet-faced server brought him, as requested, a whisky and then his meal and some wine. All was delicious, but his appetite for the food was poor, and although he ate most of it, it'd been a slow process. When she returned for his plate, he asked if she knew of the Bradstocks, and her surprise was unexpected.

Daniel stared at her. 'I'm sorry, I don't understand. Is there a problem asking for this family?'

'No. Just unexpected. Which Bradstock do you want? And why them in particular?'

'I have a friend called Sebastian Whitchurch. He's a portrait painter. He's a distant cousin of someone who used to live round here. Well, was, I suppose. I gather the other Whitchurch is deceased.'

'That would be Henry Whitchurch. Yes, he died just over a year ago. And?' Absently, the server pulled out a chair and sat, her chin on her hand, looking sympathetic.

The connection to the woman that had tugged at Daniel earlier tugged again, and he felt his defences rise, trying to guard against it. But it didn't work, and he gave in, his defensiveness washed away by their unexpected bond, and he poured out more information than he'd intended. 'I had to leave my home. It was imperative I left immediately, and I can't go back until certain issues are resolved, so I can't access my studio. I went to see Sebastian, and because I need to get some paintings done to give to my agent, he suggested going to the coast. He suggested tr-trying here...' His voice stuttered to a halt.

'Sounds like you've had a lot on your plate,' she murmured, a gentle smile on her beautiful face, her hair escaping its ponytail and curling round her high cheekbones.

Kindness. Made him want to collapse into her arms. He'd make an utter fool out of himself, though. Exhaustion slammed into him, and he erected his defences fast. He couldn't cope with kindness right now, couldn't cope with whatever it was he felt for this woman he'd just met. Better to shut it out, shut *her* out.

'Sebastian told me his relative had owned a large house, and he'd intended to leave it to some people called Bradstock. Anyway, he suggested if the family was living in the house, they might have a cottage to let, which I could rent for the summer. He seemed to recall there was one belonging to the house, which was on the cliffs nearby. I ju-just want to know where the Bradstocks live. So I can ask. F-for accommodation.' His speech becoming disjointed again, Daniel scrubbed his face, dropped his hands onto the table, and stared at the white cloth, swamped with the fallout from the last two days.

He felt the cool touch of her fingers on the back of his hand and looked up, startled. She was gazing at him with compassion.

'You're exhausted, aren't you? You poor man.'

Fuck! He couldn't handle this kindness.

'Do you know where I can find them?' His voice was sharp, and he hated himself as he saw her flinch. He felt irrationally saddened and rubbed his face with his hands again to avoid seeing her disappointment.

'Mmm, well.' Her voice had gone quiet, her eyes lost their brimming friendliness. 'Your friend Sebastian Whitchurch is a bit out of date, which isn't surprising. Henry Whitchurch left the house to Jake Bradstock, yes. Then Jake gave the house to his partner, and they used her money to turn it into a hotel.'

Daniel's eyebrows rose, and he looked about. '*Here*? This place? The Haven House Hotel?'

She nodded, her smile returning. 'Yep. Here. This place. And Jake *has* got some cottages, yes, but they're probably all let out for summer, or if they have a vacancy, it might be a week here, a couple of weeks there, and you'd have to keep shifting round.'

Daniel despairingly shook his head. Now what?

'Don't worry.' Her voice was soothing. 'There will be a room here for tonight, so you can get some sleep at least. Meanwhile, I'm sure Jake and Emily will do their best to find you somewhere.' He saw her look dubious before she smiled again. 'Let's get you booked in and we'll see what the morning brings. I'll tell Jake and Emily what the situation is. Sounds as if you're in a bit of a mess, so we'll do our best to help you out.'

'We?'

'I'm another Bradstock. I'm Claire, Jake's sister, and the gardener here. They were short staffed, so I was only serving for tonight.'

Daniel stared at her. This was his good luck for the day—that this kind, beautiful woman had been unexpectedly in the dining-room, had seen his exhaustion and distress, and was capably dealing with the current obstacles for him. Haven House Hotel—how apt the name. For now, the place was indeed a haven, and that included her.

'Thank you,' he said humbly.

'Come.' Standing, she reached out a hand, and he let her take one of his and tug him to his feet.

The warmth of her hand felt good. Her kindness was almost breaking him. His abruptness hadn't put her off.

Still leading him, she took him through some large double doors and into the lounge. Not the way he'd come in, which had been via the reception hall. A man with longish hair in a riot of loose curls stood behind a serene looking, dark-haired woman sitting at a small table. His hands on her shoulders, both were looking at a laptop open in front of them.

'Emily, Jake,' Claire said to them, 'this gentleman has a problem. First, he needs a room for the night, then tomorrow morning, he needs somewhere long-term to stay. Maybe we can sort something out over breakfast?' She turned to smile at Daniel. 'That sound okay?'

Dazed, he gave a slight nod of his head. 'Yeah. Yes. That's good, thanks. If you don't mind?' He looked at the other two. Oh, yes—his artist's eye immediately picked out the likeness between the Bradstock siblings. A good-looking pair, with the same high cheekbones and well-shaped mouths, both brown-eyed with golden glints. Claire's hair was darker and less curly than Jake's tangled, sun-kissed blonde mop, but easy to see they were brother and sister, both of them more casual than Emily… is that what Claire had called her? Emily's dark hair fell heavily to her shoulders, framing an oval face and emphasising her large, intensely blue eyes. She wore chinos and a silk shirt with a cardigan slung over her shoulders. Very smart and a bit of a contrast to Jake in his faded jeans and a pale blue tee shirt with a small tear on the shoulder.

Emily gazed at the dark stranger, a look of puzzlement in her eyes. 'But isn't this…?' Her voice died away in hesitation.

Jake smiled, stepping into the awkward pause with friendly ease. 'Yes, we've got a room spare. Emily will need to register you. Do you have any luggage?'

'My name's Daniel Morgan. I've got a bag in the car.'

'Oh!' Claire exclaimed, looking awed. 'Daniel Morgan? *The* Daniel Morgan? Seascape artist? Now I know why you look familiar!'

Daniel turned to stare at her. Her eyes were wide, and she'd clasped her hands under her chin. He knew his fame was growing, but to find a gardener here in coastal Wales who instantly knew his name, even seemed to recognise him, was a surprise. He raised his eyebrows, rubbing his chin tiredly. 'You sound as if you might know me?'

'Um, well, yes. I do. Or I should say, I know *of* you.'

He nodded.

'So only by repute, and your paintings.' She grinned. 'I'm a fan. I love your work.'

Daniel stood, looking at her. Her words seemed

genuinely meant. 'Oh. Well—thank you. Look, my bag's in the car. I'm parked just out the front. I'll get my things.' He was so tired he couldn't even process this new bit of information—that Claire the rescuing angel knew of his work. Was a fan. Turning, he went out into the cool, just-turned-dark night and pulled his bag from the back seat. He left his travelling art kit in the boot for now until he found out what would happen to him tomorrow. Just for a moment, he paused and took a deep breath. The air was warm and full of delicate smells brought out by the dew. Wet grass, flowers, the sea. Raising his eyes, he saw stars, while behind him, the solid bulk of Haven House glowed with warm lights from its windows. An element of calm seeped into him.

Returning to the entrance hall, he could see Claire in animated discussion with her brother and his partner—or was she his wife?—and he overheard Jake saying something about thinking it over before tomorrow. Emily walked over, and, fingers flicking over the keyboard of the Reception laptop, asked for his address and any other contact details as she registered him.

Daniel turned towards the stairs, and Jake offered to show him to his room. With one last lingering look at Claire, he turned and staggered with sheer exhaustion, grabbing the handrail. He followed Jake up to find his personal haven within the Haven House Hotel. What a whimsical thought. His lips flickered in a faint smile.

With a sigh of relief, Daniel undressed, showered and got into the comfortable bed. He could sort out the problems of his accommodation tomorrow, but just before he slept, he wondered if it might be best to stay here at the hotel… except it would make painting so difficult. And Claire might be a complication he hadn't expected and didn't think he wanted. This was a woman he could fall in love with. He knew that like he knew the sun would rise in the morning. He could love her with ease. If he let himself. But he wouldn't let himself.

To the sound of distant waves washing onto an unseen beach, he was instantly asleep.

CHAPTER 3

CLAIRE WAS up as dawn broke, full of nervous energy. Emily and Jake were practical, and they wanted to help. They would've considered the proposal she'd made last night, that she and Daniel shared Gardener's Cottage, and they'd probably say no. It hadn't been a terribly brilliant suggestion, Claire knew that, so she'd had another idea and was eager to communicate it before Daniel appeared for his breakfast.

That wasn't the only reason she was up early, though. She wanted to have a quick look round the gardens and grounds—or as much as she could manage before breakfast—to get an idea of the size and magnitude of the task ahead of her. After a rapid tour of the immediate area round the hotel and a look at the walled garden, she headed up to the hotel, where she found Emily already up and sipping from a cup of some odd-looking brew, sitting in a corner of the immaculate dining-room.

Leaning over, Claire sniffed. 'Ginger?'

'Ginger.' Emily nodded. 'Does wonders for the morning sickness. Your mum told me. A cup of ginger tea and a ginger biscuit.'

Claire helped herself to a cafetière of coffee from the breakfast bar and snagged a few slices of toast before re-joining Emily. 'I've just had a look round the grounds and been to the walled garden this morning. Did you know there are still traces of the old beds in some places, and in the walled garden, there's some good terracotta edging hidden under the weeds?' She waved her hand in the general direction of the grounds. 'A hand rotovator would help to re-establish the kitchen garden, then I can probably grow a few things before the summer's over. And there are three greenhouses, but they're in a terrible state of repair. To be honest, it might be best if we cleared them and started afresh, but obviously I want to run these things past you and Jake first. Also, there are still the stone steps leading down to various levels in the main gardens. From what I remember of the plans we looked at during my interview, there were different gardens all leading into each other. It'll certainly take some time—years—to fully restore everything. For now, though, I'd like to concentrate on the rose garden just below the terrace, the beds at the front of the house, and the kitchen garden.' Claire grinned, eyes shining, her enthusiasm contagious. This whole thing was going to be so amazing.

Emily took a sip of her ginger tea, smiling. 'I've already noticed in just a week you're making a real difference, so thanks.'

Claire felt pleased. As soon as the summer holiday had begun, she'd started weeding the flower beds and cutting the lawn edges in the immediate vicinity of the house. While the complete restoration would take years, there was also plenty of ongoing work to be done.

'And yes,' Emily said, 'I'd love it if we could get the walled garden up and running. We could grow some vegetables, maybe even some fruit in the greenhouse. You're going to need help, though, surely? You can't do all the gardens alone. Obviously, you'll be in charge, but you'll have to employ someone. Can you organise an advert and an interview? It has to be someone you're happy with, so no point me doing it.'

'Yes, I can do that, but…' Claire paused.

'But what?'

'Can I leave it for now? Let me get settled in and get a feel for the place? I can manage everything pretty well for now, if we have the contractors back in to keep on top of the mowing, and the trimming and pruning work. Maybe I'll start looking for someone in the summer, because there's always a lot to do in autumn, and we can start on some of the restoration work over winter. Is that okay?'

'Yes, I'm good with that, but as soon as you think a second gardener would be viable, go for it. I always intended there would be two of you. Anyway, you sound to be well in control.' Emily smiled and then her face lit up as Jake wandered over to their table.

They kissed. It was wonderful to see Jake so happy, and so much in love. It gave Claire hope for her own future. Her thoughts drifted to Daniel Morgan, an exhausted and sad man. From the moment she'd seen him standing in the dining-room, she'd been lost. Whether he felt anything in return was impossible to tell. He'd been in no state to show any emotion but distress. His manner had been a little terse and withdrawn, but he'd allowed her a glimpse beyond that, to the lonely person underneath.

'Morning, big sister.' Pulling out a chair, Jake sat down and helped himself to the coffee. 'Emily and I discussed your suggestion that this guy could share your cottage, but the answer is no. Okay, so he says he was sent here by some distant cousin of Henry's, and you reckon he's a well-known seascape artist, but we don't know what sort of man he is, and we honestly think it would be unwise for you to open up your home to an unknown quantity. It would be very awkward if you found you didn't get on.' He and Emily shared a look, and Emily gave a small nod.

Rolling her eyes, Claire took a slice of toast and buttered it. 'Honestly, Jake. I'm thirty. If I advertised for a flat share, I wouldn't know anything about the person who took the room, and I'd have the same problems. What's so different?'

Rubbing a hand over his stubbled chin, Jake looked serious. 'There's no need. He can have a room in the hostel. There's always an empty one.'

'Where would he paint? He said he needed some paintings to hand over to his agent but he couldn't access his studio.'

'Which brings us back to one reason Emily and I aren't keen on your idea. *Why* can't he access his house?

His *own* house? We know so little about him, except what he tells us.'

Claire shrugged, her mouth turning down at the corners. 'I don't know. He didn't tell me. But you could see he was at his wits' end and completely exhausted. I thought he might end up in tears at one point, to be honest. He needs the space to paint. The cottage is roomy enough, if he had the bigger bedroom. And the living room is—'

'No. And if we went the holiday cottage route, he'd have to spend some time in the hostel anyway because we don't have a long enough vacancy in any of them, so he'd have to move out of one, then into a different one throughout the holiday season. He can have a room in the hostel, or he can go elsewhere.'

Claire fell silent. Jake seemed prepared to display his down-to-earth business sense more openly these days, and she hadn't adjusted to this new version of her laid-back brother yet. She breathed in deeply through her nose, lips compressed.

Leaning forwards, Emily laid a sympathetic hand on her clenched fist. 'I think—we *both* think—you were really kind to offer. And we're not turning him away. He's welcome to stay for as long as he wants in the hostel, and we'll give him preferential rates too.' With a wink and a grin, Emily sat back.

Claire repeated what she'd said before. 'He won't have enough room. Bad enough when I paint, but he's a master.' For a few moments they were all silent, then Claire launched the alternative idea she'd come up with early that morning. 'How about *I* move into the hostel for the summer, and he has the cottage?'

Just as Emily and Jake were exchanging more looks, Claire glanced up. Her heart started a slow, measured pounding. Daniel Morgan stood hesitantly in the doorway, scanning the scattering of people having breakfast. If she'd had any doubts she'd over-exaggerated his impact on her last night, her reaction now dissipated them like morning mist when the sun came out.

He spotted them and crossed the room, allowing her to admire his easy stride. Hell, but this man had her in the palm of his hand, and it wasn't just because he was a painter. It wouldn't have mattered what his job was, truth be told. But... *why*? Was it because she sensed how unhappy he was? Was he just one of her lame ducks? She didn't think so. There was something more here, and she'd have to see what happened over the summer. Her stomach flipped as she looked him up and down. This was one very sexy man.

As he reached their table, he gave a brief smile that failed to reach his eyes and a nod of his head, then he sat on the edge of the empty chair, his long-fingered hands resting on his thighs.

'Morning, Mr Morgan.' Emily gave him a professional smile. 'Do help yourself to breakfast.' She indicated the table where guests could help themselves to cereals and toast. 'If you want a cooked breakfast, I can recommend the full English.'

'I won't have breakfast, thank you.' His voice was the same flat, tired one Claire had heard last night, and her heart sank. The moments when he'd opened up and shown her a glimpse of his inner self, and welcomed her sympathy, weren't apparent today.

'No?' Jake gave his amiable smile. 'Coffee, though? No-one refuses coffee.'

'They do if they prefer tea,' Claire interjected, smiling brightly as she glanced from Jake to Daniel.

Daniel looked at her, one eyebrow raised, before turning to Jake. 'Thanks, but no. I'm going to pay my bill and head off. I'll look for accommodation elsewhere. I realise Sebastian was mistaken, but then he didn't know about the hotel. And I don't think you've got any spare cottages, from what you said last night? Or at least, nothing long-term? I need something until the end of July. I'll definitely be leaving then because I have to go to America.'

Jake and Emily exchanged another look before Emily turned to Claire. 'What you just said—do you really mean it?'

'Not as if I've settled in yet,' she said, shrugging. 'My things are still in storage and can stay there because I had to take out a three-month block, anyway. I could stay at the hostel, or even with mum, come to that. No skin off my nose, and it solves Da—Mr Morgan's problem.'

A knot gathered between Daniel's brows. 'What?' he asked abruptly. 'What does she mean?'

'*Claire* is offering you the cottage you mentioned last night, the one by the sea.' Jake took a final swig from his cup and stood, dropping a kiss on the top of Emily's head. 'Gotta go, darlin'. The café's waiting.'

'I can't accept it.' Daniel stood as well, pushing his chair back.

Claire laid her hand on his arm. He tensed as if he might shake it off, but he didn't. He stared down at it for a long moment before lifting his head and looking at her.

There was only him and her. Everything, everyone, faded away. Claire trembled and felt light-headed as they exchanged a long glance. She wasn't imagining it. He felt something, too, she was sure.

'Think about it,' Claire said. 'This is a cottage I've slept in for less than a week. It has sea views. It's got plenty of room for canvasses and paints, and you're on the cliff path, so access to various points you might be interested in is literally on your doorstep.'

'You seem to know what I need?'

'I never mentioned it last night, but I paint myself. Landscapes and seascapes, but not at your level of ability. It's a hobby, mostly, and sometimes I sell a few in one of the local tourist shops.' Claire gave a deprecating half smile. 'It won't hurt me to use a room at the hostel or head back to Mum's for a few weeks. Doesn't matter which option I choose. I was going to grab Jake this coming weekend and get him to move some of my stuff in, but all that's in the cottage at the moment are a few personal bits and bobs and some basic foods like bread, coffee, and some milk.' She dropped her hand, flushing as she realised how long it had been on his arm.

Slowly sitting back down, he rubbed a hand across his chin and looked at her with dazed suspicion. 'Why would you do this? I'm a complete stranger to you.'

She shrugged. She wasn't sure what to say for a few seconds before deciding on some of the truth. Not all, for how could she describe her feelings, which to him would seem nothing short of ridiculous? They even seemed ridiculous to her at the moment. She needed more time to come to terms with this sudden upheaval to her ordered existence.

'I think you've had a nasty experience, and it's something to do with your house and why you can't go back there for the time being. You need some space to work. I'm being honest when I say I've hardly moved in. Your need seems greater than mine. It's that simple.'

'Nothing's ever that simple,' he muttered. 'There's always an agenda.'

'Not as far as I'm concerned.'

For a long moment he stared at her, and she met his intense gaze unflinchingly despite feeling as if a swarm of butterflies had found a new home inside her body.

'There's always an agenda,' he repeated, shaking his head, his gaze dropping as he fiddled with the unused place settings in front of him.

'Okay, maybe there is,' Claire admitted, a gleam in her eye. 'You could offer a critique of one of my paintings?'

His head shot up, his face blank. But then his expression lifted, and his mouth twitched. It completely changed his face. Just as well she wasn't standing. Her legs felt like water.

But then, like the sun going behind a cloud—and a pretty stormy one at that—the faint smile disappeared.

Emily had sat, a quiet observer of all this. Now she

stood up and smiled warmly at them both. 'Let me know what you decide, won't you? I think Claire truly doesn't mind, Mr Morgan. You look as if you've found your summer accommodation, so my advice is to accept her offer before she changes her mind. There won't be anywhere offering a long vacancy on the coast at this time of year. Okay, I'm going to get on. Probably see you later, Claire?'

She left them, and they continued to sit in silence. Claire was patient and decided there was no reason to fill it with inane repetitions, and she assumed Daniel Morgan was weighing the pros and cons of her offer and maybe his alternatives. Anyway, it gave her time to think about him.

Somehow, finding "the one" had never been high on her agenda. For years, teaching had filled her life, and she'd had a couple of good relationships, but no-one had steam-rollered her like this man did. If he stayed here over the summer, they had a chance of building something together. Maybe they could paint together… if she dared let him see her work, that was. They could go for some walks because she knew the whole coastline, north and south, for several miles. She'd really like that. But… if they did, what then? He'd want to return to his home at some point and then was going to America, while she… well, she was new to this job and wanted to prove herself, as well as create something both beautiful and useful. She wanted to stay here.

One thing she'd love to know, though—what on earth had driven him out of his house and made him so distressed?

CHAPTER 4

DANIEL PICKED up the fork from his unused breakfast place and used the handle to draw a pattern on the tablecloth, silently brooding. He'd slept well last night, and the view from his window had been more than pleasing. He itched to walk the coast with sketchbook and camera, and knew he'd get some great stuff round here. But, but, but… it meant putting himself into debt to the lovely Claire—server from last night, also related to the owners, and *also* the hotel gardener.

He shot her a surreptitious glance, his artist's eye—so he told himself—appreciating the line of neck and jaw, the thick, slightly curling hair today falling loosely over her shoulders, and her beautifully shaped mouth. His eyes dropped lower to the curve of her breasts and his body stirred in response—the same reaction he'd had last night. Hell!

Pity she wouldn't be up for a one-nighter. Sex would be so much easier than thinking of her as a potential friend, someone he could talk to or share things with.

He was too raw to let her in. He was almost, if he was honest, frightened to let her in. If he accepted her offer, would she move on him? He thought she was attracted to him, but he could have read it wrong. Besides, last night he'd been damned tired. If she was interested though, she hadn't a snowball's chance in hell of entangling him in a relationship. Yet he, too, was aware of a spark sometimes flashing between them, however unwelcome it was, and he was more than aware of his body's tentative lust.

But this place she mentioned, this cottage, which she said was on the edge of the beach, sounded ideal. It must be the place Sebastian had talked about. Her sympathy, and her kindness in giving up her home, however new it was to her, tugged at his heart and stirred emotions he'd rather leave well alone. She didn't deserve to suffer because of the emotional burdens he carried. That thought alone surprised him, but it was followed by another, even more startling. Maybe they could be friends, despite his earlier concern? Casual friends? She'd know the area and might be helpful pointing him to the more dramatic coastline. They didn't have to discuss anything personal, but stick with light, neutral topics. And he could easily push her away if she wanted anything more.

Taking a deep breath, he dropped the fork and looked up, hoping he wasn't about to make an enormous mistake, but unable to cope with any more uncertainty. 'Okay, I'll take you up on your offer. I'll even critique a painting.' Watching carefully to see what her reaction would be, Daniel was pleased she simply lowered her cup and suggested they check in with Emily at the office.

'There'll be a rent.' Claire stood up.

'I didn't expect to get it free,' he replied dryly, wondering if he was decent to stand. She was having too much of a physical effect on him, and he didn't like this softness he felt towards her.

'How much are you prepared to pay?'

'The going rate. I don't want favours.' Because favours put you in people's debt, and these days, he preferred to be independent.

He stood, used the excuse of tucking in his shirt to adjust his jeans, thankful his reaction to her had mostly died down, then followed her to Emily's office, where they sorted out a rental price.

'Go pack your stuff,' Emily told him. 'Claire will take you down in the buggy. We can leave you one, if you want? We never intended guests to be down there because of the distance, you see.'

'No need,' he replied brusquely, already moving to the door. 'I can walk up here. I assume you don't mind the car being left outside?'

'Not at all,' Emily replied courteously.

Aware of them watching him, he ran up the stairs. In his room, it only took him moments to pack his overnight bag, which was all he'd bothered with last night.

On his return, he found Claire waiting for him.

'I need some things from my car. I've got my travelling painting kit, and a bigger easel, which I keep permanently in the boot.' He didn't look at her as he walked towards the front door.

Silently, she followed him, and he felt the tenseness in his shoulders relax a little. At least she wasn't batting her eyelids and trying to make small talk.

Once in the buggy, she drove it competently down the gentle slope on the far right of the extensive grounds which led from the hotel towards the coast.

'The gardens look as if they need some attention.' Surprising himself, Daniel broke the silence.

'Mmm. Nothing much has been done to them for over a year, and even before then, I don't think Henry was bothering much. Emily and Jake got some contractors to tidy it up when the house was being converted, and I've concentrated on immediately round the house this last week. I couldn't start until the end of the school year because I was a teacher. I retrained on the side, and now I'm a gardener.'

'Obviously you prefer it?'

She gave a small snort. 'Well, yes. Otherwise I wouldn't have changed careers, now would I?'

Chastised, Daniel looked out of the side of the buggy, across a vast expanse of grass with trees on the far side. He wasn't up to normal conversation and banter.

He was aware of Claire's sideways glance. 'I'm sorry. I didn't mean to sound snarky.'

He ran his hands through his hair and shook his head. 'You weren't. It was a stupid observation on my part.'

'Yes, but you were trying to make conversation, and I shouldn't have shot you down.'

'You didn't,' Daniel said impatiently. 'I'm a big boy. Forget it, okay?'

Her eyebrows went up, and she bit her lower lip. He felt bad about his terse reply. Not a good beginning if he'd been thinking about a friendship.

Hell, he didn't know which direction his thoughts were going. One minute, he wanted to screw her. Then it was no, strike that, maybe they could be friends? That was quickly followed by perhaps she'd got no interest in him at all? Running through it all was the thought if he acted coolly towards her, he'd put her off. Ah, but no— he recoiled from that, because she was kind, and they might actually get on well…

And so it went, leaving him with no idea what to do at all. This was the first time he'd felt anything towards a woman in over two years. Having this attraction spark to life after he'd determined to avoid romantic entanglements was disconcerting and unexpected.

Damn Gina!

When they drew up outside a small, white building, his breath caught in his throat, and he slowly climbed out of the buggy, looking around him. Gulls wheeled above, white against the cerulean sky, the waves gently lapped on the nearby shore, and grass, flowers, seaweed and ozone combined to create an amazing fragrance. These things immediately soothed him. Collecting his two bags, he opened the small gate and followed the path down the side of the cottage to arrive at a small, flagged patio encircled by a low wall. Over the wall was the shore—a tumble of small rocks, a stretch of soft sand scattered with dried seaweed, bits of old rope, and the odd piece of driftwood—and then wet sand and the sea. It was stunning. It was perfect. No wonder Claire loved it so much.

Claire, who had joined him, spoke, her voice quiet as if in respect for the utter beauty surrounding them. 'The beach isn't used much because it's a two-mile walk along the cliffs from Solhaven that way, and four miles from Howgale in the opposite direction. But at low tide, you can walk on the beach from Solhaven, and it's only a mile, so you sometimes get a flurry of folk then. And, of course, hotel guests.'

'Where's the coast path?'

'It drops onto the beach at the far end and climbs back up at the other end. It's passable even at high tide, except if there's a spring tide or a storm.'

'No alternative route?'

'Yes. You can go up the side of the Haven House grounds and head over the fields behind the hotel. It adds about a mile, but it's easy walking.'

Daniel sat on the low wall, leaning back on his hands. 'You sound as if you know it pretty well.'

'I should!' Claire threw back her head and laughed. 'I grew up here, after all. This cottage was always my dream home, truth be told.'

Daniel's eyes widened. 'Then you—'

Claire held up her hand. 'I said, if you recall, I can postpone living here for another few weeks. It's not a problem, and I know it's waiting for me.'

He turned away to look over the beach. There was a

family wandering along the edge of the gentle surf, a man walking his dog, who took great delight in rushing into the sea, barking wildly, and a horse rider cantering along the small strip of hard, wet sand.

'Looks like the tide is going out,' Daniel commented.

'It is. There are some tide tables in the cottage to keep you straight.'

'I don't think I've ever come across a more idyllically situated place. I can see why you call it your dream house.'

'As a child, when I walked over here, I'd lean against that rock, see? The one over there…' she pointed to a large rock jutting from the sand. 'I'd dream that one day I'd live here, but had no idea, mind, that it would ever come true.'

Her voice had softened and a hint of a Welsh accent crept in. Daniel smiled, seeing in his mind's eye the hopeful girl. 'Was that why you became a gardener, so you could live here?' he asked jokingly, a smile lighting his dark features as he sat down on the low wall.

Claire glanced at him. 'Of course,' she replied with a grin.

'Why did you give up teaching?'

'Too much pressure on me and on the children. Learning seemed to be a matter of jumping through hoops. Diverging from the curriculum was impossible because every second of every lesson was accounted for and had to be covered. I stopped enjoying it.'

'But why a gardener?' Daniel was genuinely curious. 'Won't you get bored?'

'I think not, no. To re-create the Victorian garden is

going to take time, dedication, creativity and determination, but it'll be in my own time and on my own terms. Then I have my painting, which has been sorely neglected in the last year or two, and oh, lots of other things. No, I won't be bored, but I do think I'll start appreciating life again instead of just existing.'

It sounded ideal, and very similar to how he lived his own life. 'Victorian garden?'

'Yes. Emily wants the whole of the grounds returned to what they were like when the house was built in the eighteen hundreds. It's going to take several years before we'll complete the restoration.'

'Sounds amazing.' He was staring at her, enjoying her wide smile and enthusiasm, relaxing in the warm sunshine and lulled by the sound of the waves and mewling gulls.

Claire stepped towards him. 'Look, I'm sorry to dump you, but I have to get to work, so I'll show you round and I'll—'

'No need.' He'd talked to Claire too much and needed to back off, so he picked up the bags he'd set down outside the door. 'I can find my own way round. Just let me have the keys and you can go.'

She stared at him, clearly taken aback by his rapid mood change and abrupt dismissal. 'But I—'

'The keys,' he repeated, his mouth tightening in annoyance as she protested.

Claire lifted a hand, offering him a tight smile. 'Will you let me get a word in edgeways? I need to collect my things. You can keep any food there is—and I warn you it won't be much because I've been eating up at the hotel—but my eBook's in there, my toiletries, and a few clothes.'

He was silenced, then stepped forward and opened the door. 'Get your stuff,' he said gruffly. 'I'll wait out here. I'll sort myself out when you've gone.'

Her eyes widened, and a flush stained her cheeks at his rudeness. Her chin rose in a defiant gesture of pride, and he couldn't help but admire her. Left with little choice other than to turn and walk inside, Claire stalked off to the door.

There was a small, weathered table and two chairs on the patio, and while he waited, he sat, fighting to regain the contentment he'd felt only moments before, while he'd been talking to her.

Morosely staring over the beach at the sea, glittering in the bright sunshine, Daniel shook his head and huffed out his breath. He hadn't meant to annoy her, but he couldn't cope with being shown round because it would mean more chat. He was unused to talking these days, and he'd just about had enough. He wasn't sure he liked what happened to him when he was around Claire, and the sooner she left, the better. From now on, he'd take great pains to avoid her. Ideas of a friendship were probably unwise. He couldn't consider any kind of relationship other than a quick fuck. No involvement needed, just a release of sexual tension.

Within a few minutes, Claire reappeared, a carrier bag in each hand. 'Thanks,' she said with detached politeness. 'I need to get to work now.'

Without another word, she walked round the side of

the house and he heard the whine of the buggy's electric engine gradually fade as she drove back to the hotel.

Good. He'd got rid of her.

So why did he feel a sense of loss? Why did his self-imposed isolation seem a poor alternative? Standing, a frown on his face, he picked up his bags and went inside the cottage, shutting the door with a bang. He was still annoyed with himself for his rejection of someone who had so far been unfailingly helpful and kind.

But it had to be done. He didn't want the slightest risk of getting entangled with her. Unless she wanted that fuck, of course. Be great if she did, but women liked emotional ties, getting close, dependency. The best way to proceed, as it now seemed he'd be living here over the summer, was to freeze her out. Now.

Leaning against the closed door, Daniel tipped his head back and blew out another sigh. He hated the fact his wife had damaged him so badly he no longer believed in love. His mother hadn't been a barrel of laughs, either, and had played his father for a fool. Gina had, initially, seemed different, but as his fame had grown, she'd changed, loving being in the spotlight at events he was invited to, flirting with anyone famous. Then the affairs had started. And *then*—his thoughts came to a rapid halt. He could never contemplate her ultimate betrayal without a desire to punch his fist into something, or howl to the skies, because he was angry, and he was broken.

He wouldn't go there. *He wouldn't go there*!

Twisting his lips, he pulled away from the door and wandered through the kitchen into the good-sized living room. There was plenty of light, with large French windows opening onto the patio, and another window to the side. Upstairs were two bedrooms separated by a small bathroom.

On his return to the kitchen, he pulled open cupboards and drawers, checking what there was, and making a quick list on his phone. Before he painted, he intended to buy in some food and drive round the immediate area, see if there was anywhere which jumped out at him, to start his first sketches.

His thoughts drifted to Claire. She'd be useful as a guide, and she seemed fun.

No!

He would retreat into his customary world of solitude. That was the best way. There would be no more hurt if he kept himself isolated. And love, as he'd decided two years ago, was for fools.

CHAPTER 5

IT WAS SEVERAL NIGHTS LATER, and quite late, when Claire next saw Daniel Morgan duck his head to avoid the low lintel and step into the bar of the Ship In A Bottle on the harbourside in Solhaven. She was with a group of people who were laughing at something someone had just said, and noticed his eyes flick over them, dismissing them, until he caught sight of her and hesitated.

After a few moments, during which their gazes locked, he turned deliberately away.

A flush rising on her cheeks, the laughter fading from her face, Claire bit on her lip. Unable to stop watching him, she observed him respond to the landlord as he slid onto one of the bar stools, clasping his hands loosely in front of him. The landlord pulled a half pint and slid it in front of him, saying something which caused Daniel to smile.

The pub smelled of chips and beer, and the windows were open to the balmy evening air, chatter and laughter seeping out into the summer night. Happy holidaymakers, cheerful locals.

Another burst of laughter from her group, who were on the far side of the bar from where he sat, caused him to look up, and he met her eyes for a second time. After another few moments, when for her, the noise and people faded, leaving them both in silent communication, his head dipped in a brief greeting before he slid off the stool and carried his drink to an empty table by an open window. It was clear he wasn't interested in talking to her. She gave a quick shake of her head as the world around her slowly reinstated itself.

Daniel Morgan puzzled her. She knew him to be a man at the top of his profession, and she followed his career on various social media sites simply because she loved his style of painting. She knew he was doing well in his chosen profession. His paintings were in demand. He gave talks and lectures and was invited to openings and galas, so why was he so bloody miserable? Why wouldn't he follow up on the interest she was sure she'd detected in him on that first night? He was very attractive, too. More the outdoors type than cover model, and a sheer pleasure to watch, in his worn denims and black tee shirt, with his craggy face and rumpled black hair. Feeling her insides melt, and her heart pick up its pace, she yearned to reach out and touch his hard body, and kiss his brooding mouth… but more importantly, take the pain from his eyes.

Yet… thinking about it, in the last year, there'd been very few reports about him attending anything, and no pictures. That was probably the reason she'd thought he was familiar but not recognised him, because in previous photos, Daniel looked... different, whereas now he looked tired, almost defeated, with harsh lines bracketing his mouth. His social media feeds had dried up as well. Something must have happened to him. Something dreadful.

Claire felt drawn to him, almost viscerally, almost against her will. But she knew she'd have to break through his sadness, and find the man whose eyes had flickered with interest the first time they'd encountered each other before she would properly understand him.

Maybe she should talk to Emily, who knew what it was like to fall for someone so abruptly, because Claire had no experience of this. She'd never met someone she felt so interested in, and she'd never met someone so immune to her. Hopefully they could become friends, but it looked like that would prove more difficult than she'd first suspected.

But a friendship would be a good place to start, if she could bank down on her desire.

Despite her intention to ignore Daniel and enjoy the last half hour of her evening, she couldn't stop brooding about him. She kept looking over to where he sat by the window, probably watching the scattering of people outside. People casually walking along the harbour wall, calling out to each other, munching on fish and chips, kissing on a bench. He was watching life pass him by, keeping himself aloof, refusing to let anyone near. Well, there was only one way forward, and that was to try the friendship route.

Yes, she'd like it to be a physical relationship as well, but for now…

Unable to bear it a moment longer, and ever the optimist, she excused herself from her friends, shaking her head as someone asked her a question as she passed, and walked over to Daniel.

Slowly, he turned his head, obviously aware of her. His brows creased and his lips compressed as he stared at her without speaking. Claire felt the colour rising in her cheeks again, but she kept her gaze steady on his face as she sat down, refusing to be rebuffed.

'Mr Morgan,' Claire began in her pleasant, soft voice. 'I hope you've settled in and found everything you need at the cottage.' She paused, obviously waiting to see if he contributed something to her efforts.

He dropped his eyes to stare down at his drink. After a few moments of silence, she took a deep breath and made another attempt to reach him. 'I hope you found the milk and stuff in the fridge.'

Another long silence. Composedly, Claire took a mouthful of her wine. She'd sat with many a troubled child, waiting patiently until they finally reached out for the help they needed, and if ever anyone needed help, this man did. Daniel still seemed fascinated by the beer in his glass, but she noticed his body shifting slightly in his chair, and his hand clench on his thigh.

'Ms Bradstock,' he said finally, his voice low and harsh. 'Please don't.'

Claire felt bewildered. 'I'm sorry? Don't what?'

'Please don't fuss, don't offer any help, don't intrude, don't be interested in me.' Daniel's voice was flat, his eyes blank as he raised his head to look at her again. 'I've nothing to give, you see. Nothing at all to give.'

There could be no doubt about what he was doing. He was warning her off. Her face flushed, and she felt an unexpected sheen of tears in her eyes. Hell! She hoped he hadn't noticed. Swallowing hard, she turned her face away, again taking refuge in her wine, her turn now to stare out of the window at the passing people as she swallowed the lump in her throat. Why was she so upset? He was pushing her away, yes, but she barely knew him, so what did it matter? She bit her lip. It wasn't as simple as that. She might barely know him, but her body knew him, and her soul knew him.

She turned back. 'Not even friendship?'

'Oh, go *away*!' he muttered. 'Please, just leave me alone. I don't need a friend. I don't need you. I don't need *anyone*.'

It sounded to Claire as if he was trying desperately to convince himself he spoke the truth as he stood and drained the last of his beer before pivoting on his heel and striding out of the pub.

Claire watched him leave, her heart aching for him. Whatever he said, he needed her, or needed *someone*. Oh, what on earth had happened to him to make him so bitter about people?

Or was he simply bitter about women?

'Hey, Claire, are you coming back to join us?'

Looking up, she saw Paul, a local guy she suspected fancied her. Unfortunately, while she liked him as a casual friend, she'd no interest in him otherwise. Even before she'd met Daniel.

Standing, she drank the last of her wine and shook her head. 'Sorry, Paul. Not in the mood. I'll head off home.'

His lip curled as he tilted his head towards the entrance. 'Anything to do with that guy who just left?'

'Not really.'

But it was, and it was clear by the look he gave her he didn't believe it. 'Can I give you a lift home, then?'

'No thanks. The walk along the sands will do me good. I'll see you around.'

Neatly evading him, she set off along the beach, deep in thought. She felt it was worth just being around and trying to help Daniel. Maybe she could show him some of the best views of the coastline round here. They could certainly talk about painting and get to know each other gradually.

When Claire reached the cottage, she received a shock. In the gathering twilight of the summer evening, she observed a dark figure leaning against the low wall which encircled the patio. Realising it was Daniel, she hesitated. Did she want another encounter with him? No, it'd be best to continue along the beach until she reached the gate into the hotel grounds. But as she came level, the sound of his voice halted her.

'Not you again. I hope you weren't following me?'

Claire almost growled. Considering she'd decided to walk past, she felt the fault of this second verbal encounter lay at his door.

'You know something?' she asked equably, moving up the steps to his level. 'I think I can reciprocate. Not *you* again. I'm heading for the path up to the hotel, which goes up the same track that serves the cottage. The gate is just there, so I've every right to be passing. Public beach, as far as I know.' She was prepared to give him some leeway, but wouldn't turn herself into a doormat. 'In the pub tonight, I simply extended you the courtesy of some friendly chat, which I would do to anyone staying in the hotel.' She glanced at him, her hair tangled softly round her face by the breeze.

There was a long silence as Daniel stared back. 'I must apologise, it seems,' he finally said, reluctance in his voice.

His eyes pinned Claire. She became as helpless as a rabbit in the headlights of a car until at last, with a low exclamation of dismay, she forced herself to move, turning to drop back onto the beach.

But he moved even more quickly, stepping away from the wall and catching hold of her hand. She was aware, as she tried to pull away, of the warmth of his fingers, the faint smell of citrus aftershave and his own unique male smell. A tremor ran through her. She needed to get away from him as soon as possible, before she did something stupid, like kiss him. Her body's reactions were a betrayal of her determination to keep her attraction under wraps.

In the last of the daylight, Claire was aware of several fleeting emotions passing swiftly over his features—sadness, tenderness, maybe even regret. She couldn't be sure, but one thing she knew, he wasn't as detached as he wanted her to think.

Shifting uncomfortably, she cleared her throat.

'Look, do you mind? I'd like to get home and you're stopping me.'

Daniel laughed softly, but somehow it lacked humour. 'Why the hurry? I thought you wanted to talk to me? That's what you said you were doing back at the pub. Having a friendly chat... well, talk away. I'm here. Captive audience.'

His words grated. She knew he was using them as weapons, and it was working. They hurt. She decided it was better not to show it and maybe about time he needed someone to stand their ground.

'You're not the captive here. I am, and I object! Let me go.' Her voice was low, controlled, and full of authority.

He looked down to where he held her hand, surprise on his face, and after a few moments, he let her go. 'I'm sorry.'

'You seem so unhappy. All I'm trying to do is reach out to you, maybe offer friendship, but you make it very hard.'

She turned away and looked across the water. The rising moon cast a wide beam of light on the sea, blurring and wavering in the movement of the waves.

Daniel Morgan seemed to have the power to make her feel very emotional and for someone who considered herself calm and collected, it came as a bit of a shock he had this... this *control* over her.

'Yes, I know you are. And in some ways, I appreciate it,' Daniel said, his voice tired as he spoke to her resolutely turned back. 'But I prefer not to get involved these days, and that includes friendship.

Friendships demand a certain involvement, which I don't want to give or receive. I might find you attractive—damn you, I admit it, I *do* find you attractive—but that doesn't mean you can assume anything. Not now and probably never. The last thing I expected when I came here was something like this happening. I'm not surprised you find me so difficult to reach, and the solution's easy. To me you're just an unwanted irritation, so please, keep away from me, and —' His voice broke.

She turned back to face him, her mouth opening with shock at the pain in his words, and held out her hands. Whether he admitted it, he needed someone. He needed comfort.

Daniel retreated. 'Look... *listen* to me, damn you! Just listen! I don't trust women, and I've no intention of getting involved with someone ever again, so if you thought...' His voice trailed off despairingly.

Claire let her hands drop, his misery slicing through her. 'But you need a friend,' she murmured. 'Someone to talk to, just *be* with. It can be uncomplicated, you know. You don't have to exchange life histories with each other. We can just have fun. You know someone's there for you if you need to talk.'

He straightened his shoulders and interrupted her, his voice flat. 'I need nothing. The only time I get close up and personal with anyone these days is for a good fuck, okay? I'll say it again... I find you attractive— sexually attractive. So, okay, you say you want to help me. Come inside. I'll take you to bed. I'll even make sure you have a good time. But that would be all. I've no emotion to offer you. No love. No trust. And certainly, no commitment. I'm empty, and I'm broken.'

Before she could move, he closed the short distance that separated them and pulled her against his body, his arms snaking round her like bands of steel. 'Did you hear? Are you going to come inside with me for a good fuck?'

Claire stared at him, saw his eyes gleaming in the fitful light of the dying day. Her glance fell on his well-cut mouth with its sculpted lips, the small creases at each corner indicating humour and showing her that once, he hadn't been as burdened as he was now.

She felt no fear.

In his arms, she could only feel the need to be closer, to love him, and to soothe his distress away. Of their own accord, her hands slid up his hard chest and curled round his neck, her fingers tangling in his thick, wild hair, and she felt his lips drop, hard and demanding on her own.

His tongue ran demandingly along the crease of her lips, which she opened until their tongues touched and explored. Her stomach swooped and a cool rush passed through her body until it gathered at the juncture of her legs and changed to passionate desire. Damn, but this guy knew how to kiss!

As her tenderness met his angry despair, his kiss unintentionally softened. His hands became gentle on her hips, and his lips and tongue continued to tease hers with sensuous need. For one brief, glorious moment, they swayed in a mutually felt passion. This kiss… it told her everything her body had known—they would be good together. Their bodies were made for each other, and as crazy as it sounded, perhaps their souls too. In the press of his lips and the seeking of his hands, he dropped his defences, and she saw him, felt him, knew him.

She used her own lips, her own hands, to heal him and offer nurture to the soul he kept hidden away. If he could survive the devastating drought in his life, he would grow back and become beautiful and whole again. She clung to him with her mouth, pulling him toward her sunlight, seeking that self he hid from everyone. He should never need to hide it from her.

But as suddenly as he'd pulled her to him, he pushed her away, hands balled into fists, his voice drained. 'No, Claire. I'll answer my question for you. I don't want you in my bed. One-night stands are my rule, and I'm not going to use you. You deserve so much more. Certainly more than you'd get from me.'

She thought he was directing his anger as much at himself as her.

'Keep away, okay? I told you that before and I'm telling you again. And I don't think you and I can do the friends bit, either. I'm not fit for human company.' Turning, Daniel left her, striding through the gate, lost in the shadows as the last of the daylight vanished, and clouds drifted across the moon.

Claire caught hold of the gate. She should feel angry, but she didn't. Wrapping her arms around her body where moments earlier his arms had held her, she shivered as the memory of the tenderness of his kiss swept over her.

While something sexual attracted her to Daniel, she'd be the first to admit she cared for him as well, and wanted him happy again. Compassionate and empathetic, in the past, she'd met many people who needed help of some kind, and she'd always done her best to support them because it was her nature. None had needed her as much as this man did, though. She'd do everything she could for him, and if, as he said, nothing would come of it, then so be it. By taking him on, she realised she was possibly—no, *probably*—laying herself wide open to the greatest hurt she'd ever experienced.

She'd come to Haven House to recreate the Victorian gardens, a time-consuming and challenging project, and one she intended to put her heart and soul into. Could she also recreate Daniel Morgan? Turn him back into the man he once was?

A soft wind eddied round her, the gentle sound of the waves a constant lullaby, as she stared thoughtfully at the cottage.

It looked to her as if she'd given herself two massive challenges in her new life. Confident in achieving success with the gardens, she was less certain when it came to the man.

CHAPTER 6

Daniel tossed and turned all night, his mind filled with painful memories and wishful dreams, until he didn't know where one ended and the other began. Finally, as the sky lightened at around four in the morning, he fell asleep, and it wasn't until late morning he surfaced, feeling bleary-eyed and confused.

There was no reason on earth, he decided as he brewed some coffee, to break his self-imposed solitude. Safer to stay as he was. And unfair to inflict himself in this damaged state on such a lovely person as Claire. Even as just friends, he'd cause her misery. And as he'd realised last night, much as he knew he'd enjoy taking her to bed, he couldn't do it. She wasn't someone to be used.

A small voice nagged at him, telling him she appeared kind and caring. She might cope with him as he was. That same voice kept whispering as he made toast. What would it feel like to try again? To trust a woman without fear she would eventually desert him?

Ah, but he was afraid.

Eyes stormy, he slashed butter onto the crisped bread and dug some marmalade out of the jar with vicious stabs of the knife.

His own mother was the first to show him how faithless women could be. She'd neglected her husband for a string of affairs and was indifferent to her son, ignoring him when he came to her with paintings, toys or hurt knees. His father had done his best to give him a stable childhood and had encouraged his talents as an artist. Finally seeing sense, his father had sued for divorce and later met and married a gentle lady called Mandy. Too late for her to be a mother, because by then Daniel had been a young man, but she'd always welcomed him kindly.

Okay, so maybe women could be kind, and Claire might be one of them.

His mind drifted to his ex-wife. Blonde, stunningly beautiful, sexy as hell. She'd dazzled him and captivated him, and he'd been easy prey. It was much later he'd realised Gina had seen him as someone on the up, and had used him as a stepping stone until she met someone more famous, someone richer. Through his marriage to Gina, he'd realised he might have been seeking the love and approval denied to him by his mother, because it had slowly dawned on him she was exactly the same type. Faithless, shallow, self-absorbed and, as a result, cruel and destructive. But he'd not seen the likeness, not at first. He'd been overwhelmed, and anyway, Gina had wanted him. He was the upcoming darling of the art world, and charismatic with it, so she'd approached him with sweetness and flattery, and more fool him, he'd not seen through her until she had a ring on her finger and the affairs had begun.

But worse was to come, and it was the one thing he kept buried deep inside, and had never talked about to anyone except a counsellor he'd had a few sessions with. It had been a knife to his heart then, and was still a knife now. Losing their baby—how they'd lost it—had been harder to bear than losing Gina.

He took his coffee and toast outside to the small wooden table, bleached to grey by years of being exposed to the elements. It was another sunny day. A gentle, off-shore breeze allowed a family to fly two kites down by the edge of the sea, now on its timeless way out again. He could see waves languidly rolling onto the sand, and the air smelled of seaweed and flowers.

Flowers. No doubt courtesy of the delectable gardener, Claire Bradstock.

So was she a Mandy or a Gina?

Oh, he was fairly certain she was a Mandy, but that didn't mean he wanted to trust her or start some sort of relationship with her. His mother and Gina had destroyed that for him, and yeah, okay, now he lacked the courage to try again. Ever. Despite what he'd been told by the counsellor, that one day he'd be over it and would find someone to love again. He couldn't trust those words.

Shrugging, he bit down hard on his toast. It didn't matter. He didn't care.

He knew he owed Claire an apology for his appalling behaviour last night, when he'd been needlessly unkind. And that kiss… why, oh why, had he allowed himself to kiss her? He'd meant it as a coldly calculating insult, but a spark had flickered between them, then erupted into a blaze. He was hard now, just thinking about the feel of her body in his arms and the taste of her on his tongue.

There was a click. Looking up, Daniel observed Jake Bradstock descending the steps from the hotel gate, wearing shorts and a tee shirt. Shit! The last person he needed to see in view of the direction his thoughts were taking. Jake's presence was, though, a pretty effective passion killer.

Jake noticed him and paused, then in two quick strides he came up the steps to the cottage, swinging his leg over the wall, sitting astride.

'Hey. Have you settled in?'

'Thanks, yes.' Daniel paused before continuing reluctantly. 'It was good of Claire to give up her home for a few weeks.'

Jake eyed him thoughtfully. 'She's like that. Kind. Thinks of others. Any coffee going spare?'

Daniel raised an eyebrow. He didn't feel like entertaining a visitor, but it would be appallingly rude to say no to one of the very people who'd solved his accommodation dilemma. Anyway, it was difficult not to respond to the open smile on the guy's good-looking face.

Silently, he went inside, filled another cup, and returned.

'Lovely view, isn't it? Thanks.' Jake, now sitting in a chair, reached for the mug and took a mouthful as

Daniel sat back down.

A silence fell.

Daniel observed Jake as he gazed out over the sea. With his strong profile and tangled curls blown back by the wind, the man would make an excellent subject for a painting. If he'd pose with a surfboard, Daniel could then insert him into a scene of gathering waves and angry clouds. He was hoping to call his next exhibition People Sea and try to incorporate people doing various sea-based activities, and Jake would be a perfect model.

Eventually, setting down his mug, Jake grinned. 'You must really wonder why the hell I'm here.' Receiving no response, Jake snapped his fingers a couple of times in front of Daniel's face, his easy grin still in place. 'Hello? Earth to Daniel?'

'Eh? Oh. Sorry, I was putting you into a painting. You'd be a fantastic subject for a sport seascape. Would you mind posing on a surfboard? It can be on the sand. Then once I've got shots of you, I can wait until the right sea comes up and photograph that. From the two lots of photos, I'd put it all together.'

'On the sand?' Jake pulled a face, his eyes widening. 'Um... wouldn't it be better to take action shots and paint directly from those?'

Daniel raised an eyebrow. He didn't want someone messing around and wasting his time. He needed to work all summer to get enough paintings to send to his agent and liked the idea his theme would be based on people and the sea.

'Yes, maybe, but I don't have the time to look round

for someone who can surf and you're an ideal model because you actually look the part.'

Throwing his head back, Jake gave a wicked laugh, one eye-brow rising. 'Look the part, eh? Okay, I don't mind. Name the day. But look, I actually came by to see if you needed to talk. Claire doesn't think you're very happy, and Emily and I noticed you seemed pretty stressed out when you first turned up. We hadn't the heart to turn you away because of it, so just as well Claire came up with the idea of letting you stay here, since we were having a hard time finding a solution other than the hostel. And Claire said that'd be no good.'

Daniel opened his mouth, about to make another comment about Claire's kindness, but Jake held up a hand, forestalling him.

'Don't start thanking us again. She hadn't even moved in, apart from getting some basic stuff and setting up the bed. She won't mind a few weeks in the hostel.'

He spoke with the casual dismissal of a brother for a sister, but Daniel knew it was probably the truth from what he knew of Claire so far.

'But, I don't know, I just thought you might like to talk. We all go through some tough times, and it sounds like a tough time to me if you can't access your own house. It sometimes helps to offload.'

Daniel looked at the waves, his fingers drumming lightly on the table top. The wind stirred his hair, and he enjoyed the feel of the warm sun on his face. This place was sheer heaven, and he appreciated Jake's offer to talk. However, he intended to fob the guy's sister off at every opportunity, which might piss him off, so maybe better to keep his distance? He was used to being self-contained ever since Gina had done the dirty on him and made trusting so hard.

On the other hand, this was a bloke offering to talk, not a woman trying to get under his skin by finding out all about him, and sometimes a friend was good, especially when feeling as alone as he sometimes did. And if he explained, Jake might understand why he wanted to avoid Claire.

'Daniel?'

He made one last feeble protest. 'Look, I think it might be best to just be guest and hotelier.'

'Because of Claire?'

'What? What is this? What do you mean, because of Claire?'

'That first night, it was pretty clear you appreciated her help, and a couple of times I noticed you looking at her as if you wanted to make a move on her. She's damned keen to help you, that I know, and I'm sorry, but I think maybe she's interested in you as well.'

'I'd worked that out.' Daniel reached for his toast and took a vicious bite.

'Yeah, well, maybe you don't fancy her. I can understand that, and if that's the case, tell her.'

'I did, last night.'

'Ah.'

Putting his toast back on the plate, Daniel narrowed his eyes and tilted his head sideways. 'Ah? What's that supposed to mean?'

'I bumped into her up in the yard last night. She

seemed very quiet. Mentioned she'd just seen you down here and you seemed conflicted. If you're telling her no, then mean it.'

Conflicted. Hell, she'd nailed it there. Even as he was telling her to get lost, he'd allowed the detached kiss to turn into something more, and she'd known it.

He was so tired of this burden of distrust, and he wished he damned well could get over it, as he'd been told he would. Claire was attractive, kind, lively, friendly… oh, he could go on. Yes, he liked her, but he hadn't reached the point of risking another relationship. Earlier, he'd wondered if he was a coward, and had decided, yes, he was. Still too frightened to try again.

Jake put his coffee down. 'Yeah, right, I can see you *are* conflicted.'

'What? Why?' Daniel's response was startled.

'If you weren't, you wouldn't have looked all thoughtful and gone quiet on me.' Jake shot him another friendly grin. 'I'm good at reading people.'

Another long silence, but somehow Daniel didn't feel uncomfortable. There was something soothing about Jake's calm attitude and friendliness. He was a very relaxed man, and Daniel felt some of it rubbing off as his own shoulders lost their tension. It wasn't just Jake. He knew that. The warm air, the smells of garden and sea which seemed to intermingle, and the gentle sound of waves—they all combined to make him feel more peaceful than he had for a long time.

He rubbed a hand over his face, let it drop onto his thigh, and started talking.

He told Jake everything, starting with his mother,

moving onto Gina, and finally relating how she'd turned up in his house, pregnant and with her latest lover. How she'd refused to leave, so he'd left himself, leaving the mess with his solicitor, unable to return until they'd evicted her.

Lastly, Daniel told Jake the very worst of it, something he'd only ever talked about with the counsellor before. How they'd created something beautiful and lost it. No, not lost it. He'd had it *stolen* from him. Boy or girl, he'd never know now. The names he'd chosen remained hidden in the dark recesses of his mind, along with his initial excited imagination about bringing the child up, playing with the toddler, teaching the youngster to paint. All that was left to him was bitterness and a great, gaping emptiness inside.

Jake sat still, eyes fixed on Daniel's face, giving him every bit of his attention. When the artist fell silent, one tear tracking down his cheek, Jake stood, collected their mugs and disappeared inside, returning a few minutes later with more coffee. Daniel was grateful for his immense tact and understanding, the silent listening, with no exclamations, no interruptions, no questions.

His outpouring had been cathartic. It had only needed the right time, place and person, and this, apparently, was the perfect combination.

Jake dropped back into his chair, shaking his head, his eyes clouded. 'Well, shit. That's a devastating story, my friend. I see why you don't want any involvement at the present time. Hard to trust again after what she did.'

Both men fell silent as they drank the hot coffee. Daniel felt exhausted and hoped he wouldn't regret pouring out the entire story later on. Especially the last piece of information, the one that still filled him with such pain and grief. He hoped one day he'd heal, recover from it, but it hadn't happened yet.

'Sometimes, though,' Jake said eventually, 'your view of the world gets distorted by events which have happened to you. From the age of eleven, until I was eighteen, my dad was seriously ill with cancer, and I saw both of my parents crumble under the burden because of their deep love for each other. Took my mum a long time to get cheerful again after those seven years. And me? I was determined to never suffer the pain of watching someone I loved die. Ever. Keep it superficial. Keep it light. Love 'em and leave 'em. My ma called those girls my candy-flosses.' He threw back his head and gave a short laugh, but Daniel didn't think it was humorous—more self-mocking.

Jake's face became serious, and he looked directly at Daniel. 'You know what? I met Emily, and I loved her enough to want to risk it, in the end.' Waving his hand dismissively, Jake stood. 'Now, while one person has let you down badly—well, okay, two—there are still hundreds out there you probably could put your faith in. Think about it, because my bet is one day you'll look back on this as a pretty terrible episode in your life, yeah, but there'll be someone beside you who's helped you get past it. I'm going for my run now. I don't know if you run, but most mornings you can find me on the beach or one of the local lanes, and you'd be welcome to join me. Hey, how about you ask Claire to bring you over to Silver Sands tomorrow? There's a wind coming up tonight and there'll be some surf running. I'll, er, stand on my surfboard for you and you can take some photos, okay?'

With a flip of his hand, grinning as he hopped over the wall, Jake Bradstock jumped onto the beach and was soon a distant figure as he ran towards Solhaven. Daniel stood staring after him.

Ask Claire to take him to Silver Sands tomorrow? That had been sneaky, and he wasn't sure he wanted to follow through. In fact, he fully intended not doing so. Apart from anything else, she probably had a load of things she needed to be doing without ferrying him around.

CHAPTER 7

THE FOLLOWING MORNING, Claire awoke in her spacious room, tucked away under the roof of the old stables, a skylight providing plenty of light, another window looking over the gardens at the side of the house.

It was through the skylight she could see heaped clouds racing across the sky. The wind, which had come up overnight, was still blowing in from the west, but patches of blue sky gave promise of a fine day. As it was her day off, she wanted to go over to Silver Sands and maybe surf a little. While her surfing was nowhere near as good as Jake's, he'd patiently taught her the basics, and she could ride a board competently. This was the best weather for it since her return home and starting her new job. It wouldn't hurt to have lunch at the café, either. She was a great fan of her brother's cooking!

It didn't take long to shower and dress, then toast a couple of slices of bread. The one thing she missed in her cute hostel room was the inability to take her breakfast outside. But it was only for the summer.

Daniel would have to return to London at some point, and no doubt re-possess his house. She shook her head in puzzlement over that. So strange he couldn't get into his own home.

Throwing wetsuit and a towel into a bag, Claire tied her hair back into a low ponytail and was ready to go. As she moved towards the door, she noticed a square of paper on the floor. A note? Weird. Why not send a text? Opening it, she saw, scrawled in her brother's writing, a message. *Your artist mate wants to take photos of me standing on a surfboard, so I told him to come over to Silver Sands today and you'd bring him. No good texting—left my phone somewhere yesterday. Come over this morning and then stay for lunch on the house. Let's give him an uncomplicated day. J xx.*

What? When had he arranged this with Daniel, and more to the point, why hadn't he told her last night?

But she knew why—because she would've probably said no after Daniel'd told her to keep away. Especially after that kiss. Now Jake had dropped her into it. She could hardly not turn up if Daniel was expecting her. Her face set in a frown, she ran down the communal stairs and into the courtyard. A buggy was parked up by the kitchen door with a key in the ignition, but there was no sign of Jake's 4x4, so no good tracking him down and accosting him, telling him to take Daniel to Silver Sands himself. What the hell was her little brother up to?

Yet despite her mental scolding of her brother, the butterflies had started their wild dance inside, the palms of her hands were slightly damp, and her heartbeat was faster than normal. She was determined to hide all this from Daniel. He needed a friend. That was something she certainly could be, as long as she ignored the attraction that hummed insistently in her mind.

Muttering under her breath, she threw her kit into the back, started up the buggy and drove down to the cottage. Slipping through the side gate, she walked round to the patio. Daniel was there, engrossed by his eBook, a cup of coffee on the table beside him. There was also, interestingly, a piece of paper tucked under the mug to stop it from blowing away.

'You're keen, sitting out here in this wind,' Claire said abruptly, hands on hips.

'And good morning to you, too,' he replied mildly, closing the cover over the screen and standing up. 'Look, before we go any further, there's something I want to say. I shouldn't have said the things I did on Friday. And I shouldn't have kissed you. It was inappropriate, and I'm sorry.'

Claire was taken aback. Indeed, the apology was in order but she'd not expected it, and was very pleased to hear him admitting his behaviour had been wrong. Her mind darted, wondering what to say. In the end, she settled on honest simplicity.

'I appreciate your apology. I maybe also said things I shouldn't, and assumed too much, so I'm sorry, as well. Let's forget it, okay?'

He gave her a small smile. 'Okay. Thanks. Look, I gather you're my transport over to Silver Sands. I would've contacted you to say don't bother because I can find my own way there, but I don't have your mobile number, and apparently your brother has, um, conveniently lost his phone. If you can give me five, I'll collect my stuff.' Turning, he left her standing on the patio.

Edging nearer the table, Claire looked surreptitiously at the windows of the cottage, then pulled the piece of paper from under the mug and quickly opened it.

Hey, Daniel. This morning would be great for your photos, and I've located a board. I asked Claire to bring you down because she said she was coming, anyway. Can't re-arrange things because I've lost my phone and anyway, don't think you've got my number. See you later. J.

The little toad. He'd set them both up.

She folded the paper and slipped it back under the mug. Claire still felt annoyed with Jake and yet couldn't help smiling at what he'd done. So happy in his own relationship, he'd turned to playing matchmaker. But it was taking a risk, as Daniel hadn't seemed overjoyed to see her. Still, his apology was a surprise and very welcome. Maybe they could start afresh today.

She turned to look across the beach. The waves were dumping on the shore, the foam creaming up over the sand, and the gulls wheeled and turned over the sea, which at the moment was greyish green rather than blue, with whitecaps dancing over its surface. Not a day for any but the expert. Claire hoped no foolish kids would try going out on an inflatable.

'Right, I'm ready.'

Claire jumped and turned. She'd been so lost in her thoughts she'd not heard Daniel return. He had a camera bag and a lens bag slung over his shoulder, and by his side a slim leather case which probably contained a sketch pad, some pencils and a small easel. He looked thoroughly sinful, wearing a close-fitting, black sweatshirt and faded denim jeans which moulded the length of his legs to utter perfection, as far as she was concerned. Beautifully packaged, and she couldn't help think about what was underneath, despite her determination to be more restrained.

Determinedly banishing her lustful thoughts, Claire gestured to his camera. 'You take your photography seriously, then? I thought maybe you'd just take phone snaps and paint from those?'

'I need excellent picture quality, so if I can't get out, I can blow the picture up to see detail. Phone snaps are too grainy for that. It's a back-up, but I enjoy photography as another art form, anyway. I sometimes get enlarged prints made.' He followed behind her as she led the way round to the buggy, his tone carefully neutral. 'Look, why don't I travel in my car? I don't suppose you want to go, anyway, and I don't want to impose on you.'

Oh. Not necessarily a fresh start then. But he hadn't said he definitely didn't want to go with her. You could classify it as politeness and not wanting to be a nuisance. She needed to reassure him while keeping it casual and light-hearted. She realised he needed to relax and to view her an unthreatening. Once he accepted her, she hoped they could move forward.

'Ah, well, that's where you're wrong. Jake knew I'd be going this morning. I've only been to Silver Sands once since I got home, and I love that beach. And the café. Jake's offered us lunch on the house.'

'Jake has? That's very generous of him.' The surprise was clear in both his voice and raised eyebrows as he flicked her a glance.

'Yep. He owns the place.'

'I thought he owned the hotel?'

They arrived at the car park and Claire grabbed her bag from behind the buggy seat, crossing to a hatchback. Opening the boot, she dropped her kit in and gestured for Daniel to add his camera to the pile. 'Hop in. Silly to take two cars. Bad for the environment and all that.'

She was pleased to see him put his things alongside hers, accepting the lift with no more protest.

Once seated in the car, Claire answered his earlier question. 'Henry left the house *and* café to Jake. He took a shine to him. Substitute son, and maybe not a bad thing, because our dad was very ill for a long time. Sponsored him and got him working in the café as well. Jake gradually moved up and took over. Emily wanted the house for a hotel, and when they took up together, he turned it over to her. I guess they both own it, but Jake's refused to work there, apart from doing cakes for afternoon teas.'

'Cakes?' Daniel looked slightly bemused.

Grinning, Claire shot him a glance. 'Yeah, I know. He doesn't come across as a cake-maker, either, does he?'

'No. No, not at all. I'd had him pinned as a bit of a playboy type with those looks.'

Claire let out a peal of laughter. 'Oh, great. I love it. No, Jake's worked damned hard all his life to achieve what he has. Still keeps in training, too. And he's a fantastic cook. You'll find out at lunchtime. He has more help these days and spends some of his time at the hotel, but basically he still runs the café.'

The atmosphere between them had warmed from indifferent to tepid, and Daniel relaxed in his seat as she drove from the hotel to the Silver Sands car park and beach.

Once there, she jumped out, looking at the sea. There was a good swell a hundred yards from the shore, which was running sweetly until it reached the shallows. There, it rolled, foamed and heaved itself around, causing shrieks of delight from the people attempting to swim. The lifeguards were on duty and had designated an area for surfers. A few body boarders bobbed fairly close in, sometimes catching the rush of a wave towards the shore and looking triumphant as it swept them in.

'Plenty of photo opportunities for you here,' she said over her shoulder. She was buzzing with excitement and sheer joy at being back on her beloved beach and could hardly restrain herself from rushing off to change. 'Come on. Let's go find Jake, and I need put my wetsuit on.'

It was pure holiday, with families, windbreaks, kites, frisbees and the sun breaking through, lighting up the waves and the sand. Low cliffs backed the whole beach, and rocks were strewn at the bottom where small caves tempted the explorer.

Claire collected her kit from the car and rushed off to the café, not bothering to wait for Daniel.

'Jenny!' Claire almost ran towards a motherly lady who was about to go behind the counter.

At the sound of her name, the lady stopped and turned, a welcoming smile breaking across her face, her arms held wide. 'Claire! Welcome home. So good to see you.' She turned slightly towards Daniel, who stood awkwardly behind Claire. 'Hello, young man. Any friend of Claire's is welcome. My, my—you're well kitted out with camera stuff.'

'Daniel's an artist, Jenny, staying at the hotel. Well, he's renting Gardener's Cottage for the summer, and I've gone up to the hostel. He takes photos so he can paint directly from them if the weather doesn't allow him to get out. Or if the scene is likely to change too quickly, then he can start a painting and finish it from photos taken at the same time. I think?' Claire turned to Daniel, looking apprehensive.

'Yeah, you've summed it up well.' He gave her a brief smile, then looked beyond her, his eyebrows going up. When Claire turned, she saw her brother, his hair covered, and a large apron wrapped round his lean torso.

'Ahhh,' Claire said. 'The man himself. You, my lad, have got some explaining to do. But it'll keep 'til later.'

Jake grinned and unwrapped the apron. 'Breakfasts are all done, Jenny, and lunches all defrosted. You've got Angelina waiting on. Okay if I go let Daniel take some photos? He wants me to pose with a surfboard.'

Claire spun round, her happiness making everyone,

even Daniel, smile. 'I'm going to get changed. See you on the beach in five minutes, okay?'

She left them to it and went round the back of the café where Jake had recently installed some changing facilities, and a couple of showers, as well as updating the toilets. Wriggling into her full-body wetsuit, she left the back-zipper dangling and went to collect a board from the hire ones. Choosing one according to her height, she tucked it under her arm and jogged down the wooden ramp, over the soft sand and across to the surfers' section of beach.

Jake must have been quick. He was already on the beach, wearing a shorty wetsuit, his hair blowing back in the wind. His board was on the sand, and he was fooling around, striking the silliest of poses and wobbling as Daniel patiently tried to get him to lean forwards or backwards and look natural.

'Oh enough!' Claire strode over to them, frowning, and slapped at her brother's arm. 'Enough!' Casting a look of apology at Daniel, she shook her head. 'Wipe your memory card now. This idiot is wasting your time!'

Daniel was laughing. 'I'd wondered. It's clear he's clowning around. Does he even know what to *do* with a surf board?'

Where had the gloomy man who had arrived at the hotel a week ago gone? Surely that man, the one who kissed her then snarled at her, would dislike her brother's idiocy? But Daniel was amused and seemed more sunshine than storm cloud.

Her heart thumped in her chest as he leaned

forwards to say something to Jake. He was a changed man when he let go of his misery. Someone she'd very much like to know better.

'Which would be best for you?' Claire asked, stepping over to him and laying her hand on his arm, strong and muscled under the thin sweatshirt. 'Jake on his board here, or Jake surfing?'

Daniel froze, then slowly looked down at her hand and back up, his grey eyes meeting hers in bewilderment. By touching him, she'd breached his armour. And this was the second time she'd done it. Hesitating, she left her hand there just a moment longer before slowly withdrawing it.

Oddly, it felt more significant than the kiss they'd exchanged.

'What? Surfing out there? Jake can't…' His voice trailed off as he looked between brother and sister. 'Have you two been winding me up?'

'Not Claire,' Jake said promptly. 'It's me, and I'm sorry. But when you asked me yesterday if I could pose, and you said on a board on the sand, I couldn't resist.'

Claire almost growled at her brother as she picked up his board and thrust it at him. 'Go away. Stop messing Daniel around. Let him take his surfer photos, okay?'

Jake took the board and, still grinning, patted Claire soothingly on the shoulder. 'Yes, miss.'

'Put your camera on its multi-shot setting,' she advised Daniel. 'Take off your trainers and come see.'

He abandoned his trainers and rolled up the legs of his jeans, then she led him down to where the foam crept onto the beach, dragging with it pieces of seaweed torn loose by the storm out at sea.

He fiddled with his menu settings, looked up at the sky and fiddled some more. 'I hope this is going to be worth my time? I would've been more than happy to take his photo on the beach if he'd stood still. It's easy enough to take photos of any surfer and superimpose Jake's face and body. Anyway, where the hell has he got to?'

Shading her eyes, Claire stood on tiptoe and watched the heaving swells further out before flinging out an arm and pointing. 'He's just taking a wave and standing. Look—can you see him?'

It was a pleasure to watch Daniel's initial scepticism turn to open-mouthed awe. He stood, without even lifting his camera, as he watched her kid brother in his graceful twists, turning the board effortlessly to take full advantage of the water with a twitch of his hips or flex of his knees. She smiled at his gasp when Jake flipped over in a somersault.

'He really was winding me up, wasn't he?' His voice was accusing, but he was grinning when he turned to her.

'Bad habit he's got, winding people up. Next time he makes a run, get your photos. The conditions are pretty good for summer. We can go days with no real surf.'

An hour later, both Bradstocks had finished their surfing, and walked up the beach with Daniel, who was enthusing about the painting he intended to do. Watching him as he talked animatedly with Jake, Claire felt herself melt completely, and her body reacted as she occasionally bumped a shoulder against his, when the wind caught her board and made her stagger a little. Always attractive, now he dazzled with his animated face and hand gestures.

Another gust caught her, and this time he reached out to steady her, his hand firm on her upper arm.

'You okay?'

'Hard walking with the board.'

'Would you like me to take it?'

'No, all's good. We're nearly back. I'll drop it off in the rack and get changed.' Claire was looking forward to lunch with this new Daniel very much indeed.

Leaving Jake and Daniel chatting, she slotted her board into the rack, and when she turned back, she was amused to see a lady trying to open her boot and juggle a toddler, a baby, and a pram. Jake had been designated to fold the pushchair, which Claire thought would be a useful learning curve in view of his impending fatherhood. Then the lady turned to Daniel and said something with a grin.

It puzzled Claire to see Daniel step hastily back, his hands lifting, palms out. The classic "not me" gesture. Moving closer, Claire heard the lady speak.

'Look, your friend is doing a great job with the buggy. Just hold Sam for me a moment while I open the boot, okay? I promise you he doesn't bite. No teeth, see?' She let out a peal of laughter.

Daniel looked distraught and Claire was aware Jake was watching him, concern on his face as he grappled with the buggy, now half-folded. She would have offered to take the baby herself, but she was dripping salty water, wearing a cold wetsuit. Daniel, at least, was in dry clothes. About to move forwards, she halted as Daniel reluctantly nodded and allowed the tiny child to be placed in his arms. Still watching, she noticed his face change from agony to wonder, then she saw the moment his smile broke out as he bent his head closer to the baby. A small frown crossed her face. Why had he been so reluctant? Why, more to the point, had Jake looked concerned? Was it simply both were afraid to comply with the request made by the lady because of sheer lack of experience? Or was it something more?

CHAPTER 8

DANIEL LOOKED up and caught Jake's eye, giving him a brief smile of reassurance before dropping his gaze down to the baby again. He could hardly believe it. He was holding a baby, and instead of dismay, anger or anguish, he was enjoying the unexpected encounter, the feel of the tiny human, the size of him in his arms. He slowly relaxed and took in the miniature hands waving around, swore the eyes focused on him, and the baby smiled.

All too soon, it seemed, the lady smiled her thanks and took the baby back to settle him in his car seat as Jake lifted the buggy into the boot. The toddler had been standing next to her mum, thumb in her mouth while all this was going on. Jake crouched down and said something to her which Daniel didn't hear because his eyes were still fixed on the baby.

'How old is he?'

'Three months.' His mother straightened up from fastening various buckles—it seemed to Daniel to be an awful lot—and smiled again. 'Come on, Lisa. Time to go home.'

Standing, Jake approached the toddler's mum. 'Hi. I own the café here, and I wonder if Lisa might like to choose a toy from the basket there.'

He nodded his head towards the net baskets in front of the café, containing balls, buckets and spades, frisbees, and kites.

The woman looked dubious.

'Honestly.' Jake grinned. 'They cost me pennies, although I shouldn't let on about that. And I'm practising, because my partner and I are going to have a baby around Christmas.'

Daniel stepped back. Jake was going to be a father? He'd not mentioned it yesterday when they'd been talking. But then, he supposed it was hardly the right time to come out with something like that after what Daniel had told him. He turned away from the chat between Jake and the woman, looking back at the beach. The warm place in his heart caused by holding the baby was replaced with a cold vacuum.

He became aware of someone behind him and a hand on his shoulder.

'Daniel?' Jake said. 'Lunch, okay? I'm sorry you got caught up in that. Did holding the baby upset you?'

Daniel hesitated then shrugged. 'Not while I was holding him, but afterwards, yeah. It brought it all home. Enough now, okay? I'm actually enjoying my day, so let it go.' It amazed him to find it was true. He *was* enjoying himself. Watching Jake surf had been a revelation, and as they'd walked up the beach, Jake had told him about his pro surfing days, which had been both astonishing and fascinating. Even Claire had surprised him with her skill. Obviously not as good as her brother, she was graceful and competent, and he'd taken a few shots of her as well. 'I hear you're treating us to lunch?'

At that moment, Claire, her long hair wet and now nearly as curly as Jake's, joined them, a laugh on her lips and her eyes glowing. 'Treating us, and cooked it as well.'

'Hey, no, hang on!' Daniel nudged her with his shoulder, enjoying her good humour. 'You said it was cakes he made?'

'Cakes, dinners, soups… doesn't matter what, Jake cooks it.'

'Talented man, your brother.' They walked side by side towards the café.

'He is.'

'You're very proud of him. But he was given a lot.' Daniel swung his hand to encompass the café and car park. 'This and the house.'

'He worked damned hard for it. Trained day and night, worked in the café from the age of twelve as a washer-up. Henry didn't let him have it easy. Not much fun for him to have his career cut short, either. Anyway, Jake will always share what he has with his family. He is sharing it—mum works as the housekeeper, and now I've been taken on to restore the gardens. He's generous, is Jake.'

Watching her as she talked of her brother's good

fortune with a complete lack of envy, Daniel thought it wasn't only Jake who was generous.

They entered the café where Jenny had already pushed a couple of tables together, near the plate-glass windows. Emily and another woman were waiting and smiled at them both as they came in and sat down.

'Tell me more about this restoration,' Daniel said. 'You've mentioned it before, if I remember?'

'It's an amazing project to have dumped into my lap. Emily's got the original plans from when the house was built in the eighteen thirties, and I've had a look. There's so much has been removed or allowed to grow wild. Masses of work to be done. It'll take years.'

She sounded thrilled about the amount of work facing her.

'Have you ever heard of those gardens in Cornwall that were restored? This is a smaller project, but we have exactly the same elements—a kitchen garden, themed gardens opening out of each other, fountains, sea views, and there are a couple of ponds in the woods. When they were put in, the trees were planted as copses but they're very overgrown now. That will be another aim—to clear the woods down to plantations and get the ponds back to life.'

Her face grew animated as she explained, her hands gesturing wildly, outlining things she could see in her mind's eye. She was a happy woman and, contrary to his assumption she'd taken on an undemanding job instead of the more challenging job of teaching, it seemed she might have actually given herself a bigger task, and one with a lot of responsibility.

'How will you manage all this on your own?' He had forgotten his determination to keep himself aloof, in his growing interest. And not just interest in the project. In her, too. In fact, he liked Claire as a person. He liked her a lot.

'I'm not going to. Emily's said to advertise for another gardener, but I've postponed that until I can get everything straight in my head. I can't employ someone else and be bumbling around without a clue what I'm doing, now can I?' She grinned, her eyes shining.

'You all right there, Daniel?' Jake sat down on his other side. 'She's a bit nuts when she gets going about her precious gardens. Come to that, so's Emily. They really want to restore the grounds back to their original Victorian state.' He glanced affectionately at his partner, who was chatting away to Jenny and the other lady, both now sitting at the table, making them a group of six. 'You met Jenny earlier. The other lady is our mum, Annie. She's the housekeeper at the hotel, so you might see her around. In fact, I think she wanted to ask you if you wanted housekeeping—you know, cleaning and sheets and towels and stuff. After all, the cottages get a weekly clean and change of linens, so you should as well.'

Daniel looked startled. 'Hadn't even got that far, but yes. Yes, that would be great, thanks.'

'No problem.' Daniel heard Annie call out to her son. Jake gave his amiable smile, and stood, walking round the table to sit down next to her.

Still thinking about Claire and her gardens, Daniel

turned back to Claire and smiled. 'I'd love to have a look at the plans for the garden sometime.'

'Surely. I have a small office in the walled garden, and I keep everything there in a safe. Come over tomorrow sometime? Late-ish, maybe around lunchtime? I think one of the biggest challenges is in restoring the fountains. None of them were very big, but they were integral to a themed garden's design.'

Angelina interrupted them then, shyly presenting them with a menu each.

'Bit posh, Jake,' Claire called across to her brother. 'When did you start with the menus? I thought it was all written on the chalk boards?'

'Since we got in more wait staff,' Jake responded. 'Easier not to have everyone wandering round. There's usually two people in all the time, now. It's more efficient.'

There was a silence as everyone looked at what was on offer. Claire put her menu down quickly. 'No need to agonise. I want your moussaka. Daniel, I really advise you to try it—it's divine.'

Daniel looked doubtful. The last time he'd had moussaka was in Greece, and he wasn't sure anything could better that.

Jake laughed. 'I can see by the dubious look on your face, my friend, you're not sure I can cook.'

Apologetically giving a half-smile for his evident doubt, he put his menu down. 'Okay, I'll go along with Claire's recommendation. But yeah, I'm having a bit of a hard time equating the playboy Jake, which is what I first thought you were, with the champion surfer with the cake maker extraordinaire. And now the chef!'

A general laugh ran round the table before the chatter started up again. Other patrons of the café were clearly curious about the group, although a couple had waved as they'd sat down, and Jake had wandered over to have a word with them before re-joining them all.

The moussaka, when it turned up, was everything Claire had promised, and feeling genuinely hungry for the first time in months, Daniel ate the lot, inwardly admitting it was actually better than his Greek memory.

He sat back and looked round the table at the Bradstock family, together with Emily and Jenny. What a relaxed and happy crowd they seemed. And yet he'd understood Claire's and Jake's dad had suffered a long illness, lasting several years. Apparently, it had taken Annie years to recover from her husband's death, and Jake had spent most of his adult life running from one girlfriend to the next, terrified of commitment, but in the long run, it seemed none of them had let it warp them, or make them bitter. They'd recovered. Got over it. Were leading fulfilled and happy lives. Maybe the hardest bit was letting go of the past and trusting again, allowing people close once more.

He glanced at Claire. She'd offered to be there for him. She'd courageously thrown in one job and re-trained for another, which had brought her an amazing challenge. Today, she'd talked to him easily, and he felt comfortable with her. If they could both keep things like this… he looked away, biting his lip. All very well thinking that, but what about his traitorous body? He might like her on a cerebral level, but his body had different ideas and wanted to know her on a carnal level as well.

The meal continued, followed by a walk along the beach. Daniel was stunned by the simple beauty of the mile-long sands backed by low cliffs with green-clad hills, dotted with white-painted cottages. More of his accumulated tension seeped from him as he and Claire wandered side by side, and he talked of his painting.

'The next exhibition is in the autumn of next year when I return from America. I want to call it People Sea, but not see as in look. So I want paintings which incorporate people and the sea together. Like Jake surfing. Maybe some children building sand castles. Fishermen. Are there any fishing boats at Solhaven?'

'Lobster boats, mainly. But they can look good when they're coming in at sunset on a high tide. You'll have to check, but I think maybe in a week or two. What about walkers gazing down from the cliffs?'

'Could do. What sort of scenes do you like doing?'

'Oh.' Claire shrugged deprecatingly. 'Simple stuff. A bit of cliff, the shore, a couple of seagulls. Landscapes, as well.'

'I meant it when I said I'd critique one of your paintings for you.'

Claire walked on in silence for a few moments. 'There is one…' she began slowly. 'It's not finished yet. In fact, I was hoping to get out very early tomorrow and do a bit more with it. It's an early morning scene.'

'Great minds.' Daniel smiled. 'I was planning on

getting out at dawn myself. The light's always so good then, isn't it?'

She answered with a nod, and they walked in companionable silence.

What was it about this place, this family, Claire, that made him behave almost… normally? To forget hatred and betrayal and just take them—her—as they were. Friendly. Enjoying life. He'd watched Emily and Jake during the meal and seen their obvious love. He liked the way Jenny and Annie were easily included, friends not only with each other, but with everyone there. Haven House Hotel and grounds were ordered and peaceful, the café bustling and popular, and both were happy places.

It had been sheer chance that had brought him here, and he'd nearly thrown it away on his first morning by announcing he'd find accommodation somewhere else, but Claire's offer had tempted him to stay, just for a little while. At first immensely defensive, he'd attributed too much to her kindness and made assumptions she was like Gina. He'd been a pain, if he was honest. Now he'd calmed down, maybe they could be friends after all? Talk more about art and the gardens?

Today had shown him there was still enjoyment to be had from life.

Was this his first, tentative step?

CHAPTER 9

Waking very early the following morning, as he'd planned, Daniel set off to walk along the cliff path in the opposite direction to Solhaven. Jake had told him there was a small hamlet just past the cliffs, called Porthcove, with a tiny harbour and a scattering of houses, and three miles beyond that was Howgale, another good surfing beach.

From the cottage, he could see the cliffs rising sharply, with a steep drop to the sea, which had waves crashing against the base. It looked dramatic. Could he use the scene in a painting, maybe with a few people standing, indistinct in form, gazing down at the waves, as Claire had suggested?

It was a glorious morning with a clear sky; the sun rising on his left as he walked, and a steady breeze whipping his hair back from his forehead. This wasn't a stroll—the cliff path twisted and turned, dropped and rose, and sometimes went very close to the cliff edge, so he was grateful for the onshore wind. Breathing in the salty air, Daniel felt close to content. Sebastian had been right when he'd said he'd like it here.

Yesterday had… astonished him. He'd simply let go and enjoyed himself and as a result, he'd found talking to Claire easy, both during lunch and for most of the afternoon. Nor had it been spoiled when she drove him back. The casual friendliness had continued, and she had left him to walk down to the cottage with a casual wave as she took herself off to the hostel.

It seemed they could be friendly together, and yet Daniel's mouth tightened as he remembered when Claire had placed her hand on his arm, and the shock of electricity which had run through his body just from that one touch. A shock which had been repeated later, when he'd caught hold of her to steady her. A connection. Lust. But those were the things he felt unable to handle yet. They needed too much emotional investment, and he needed more time to heal.

He needed to aim for friendship with her for now. Easy enough, because they'd only ever see each other occasionally. Occasionally? Ha! He was already putting the lie to that by going to the walled garden this afternoon to look at the garden plans.

When he reached the highest point of the path, above the cliffs with their dramatic necklace of spray, foam and water, he admired the view along the coast, seeing in the far distance a long beach. It looked to have a mist hovering over it, likely caused by the spray blown from the tops of the waves, and he assumed it was

Howgale. Below him, tucked in the lee of the cliffs, was the small port Jake had mentioned, with some brightly painted boats swaying lazily at anchor and a few grey, stone-built houses surrounding the harbour in a haphazard cluster. It was perfect, and sometime soon, he itched to go further and get down to Porthcove to paint the harbour. Although there had to be a road, which would be the easier option, he decided.

After a few moments, Daniel turned, ready to go back, looking forward to some coffee. In the distance, he saw a figure running towards him. He wondered if it was Jake on a very early morning run, but before he could decide, the figure disappeared behind a high bank, and oddly, never reappeared. Shrugging, Daniel assumed there was a path cutting up through the fields.

But when he rounded the bank, he didn't find a path with a disappearing runner. Instead, he found Claire, lying spread-eagled in the dust, various items scattered round her. What appeared to be an artist's case had burst open, its contents scattered near a horribly damaged piece of thick, water-colour paper.

He ran forwards, shock freezing him to the bone. She wasn't moving.

'*Claire*! Claire, are you all right?'

She didn't move, and he squatted on his heels, reaching towards her and gently brushing the hair off her face. 'Hey, Claire! Claire, are you okay?' A note of panic entered his voice when she didn't respond.

Her eyelids flickered, and he let out a relieved breath. One of her hands lifted before dropping back into the dust, and finally, her eyes opened. After a few moments, she slowly pushed herself upright and reached to push back the tangle of hair that had fallen over her face. She winced. Quickly pulling her hand away from her forehead, she stared at the blood on her fingers in confusion.

She lifted her gaze to meet Daniel's and stared at him blankly. Looking round, some understanding seemed to return, and she blinked furiously to clear tears from her eyes.

'Hey, hey, steady. Here.' Daniel, still crouched beside her, proffered a tissue, crumpled but obviously perfectly clean. She looked a mess. White as a sheet, with blood trickling down one side of her face, and clearly very dazed. Daniel bit on his lower lip. Would she be able to stand?

Claire took it and dabbed gently at her forehead, sucking in a sharp breath as she found the cut on her head. 'I-I'm… okay,' she stammered.

She was shaken but hopefully not too seriously injured, and Daniel's heart gradually slowed its frantic pace. When he'd realised who it was lying on the gravelled path, his stomach had lurched with fear. The blood on her face was getting worse, and it frightened him, but he could see the cut wasn't too severe. Head wounds always bled a lot, he'd been told. He felt the tremble in his hands and fisted them on his thighs to control it.

Because she looked so shocked and miserable, he wanted to pull her into his arms and comfort her, but he tamped down on that feeling. He needed to be practical and get her to Gardener's Cottage to care for her injuries.

'Oh!' Claire exclaimed in further distress. 'M-my painting!' She gazed unhappily at the canvas lying face down on the dusty path, angled ominously over a protruding stone.

Daniel rose to his feet and crossed to where the picture lay. He bent and flipped it over, looking at it for a long, silent moment before picking it up and carrying it back to Claire, still sitting on the path. He put it down gently beside her.

'Oh!' This time, her exclamation was one of extreme dismay as she looked down at the jagged tear running across it.

Moving off again, Daniel collected tubes of paint, brushes, sponges, a couple of small plastic palettes and a bottle of water which lay scattered over the ground, carefully replacing them in the wooden case.

'The case isn't damaged. One corner's a bit scratched, but that's all. I think I've found all your stuff.'

He finished putting in the last few things before closing the box and placing it alongside the painting.

A tear finally escaped and rolled down Claire's face, dropping onto the now ruined canvas.

'What's the matter?' he asked worriedly. 'Are you hurt? More than we can see, I mean,' he added hastily, acknowledging the apparent damage visible was quite enough to merit Claire being called hurt, *and* cause some tears.

'N-no. No, I said I was all right. I'm sorry.' Claire

rubbed the back of her dusty hand across her eyes, leaving a smudge of grime on her nose and cheek.

'Your knee!' he breathed, his voice shocked.

Claire looked down. Blood seeped from a jagged cut liberally smeared with gravel and dirt. 'Oh, that.' She waved a hand dismissively at her knee 'That'll mend, and my head will mend.' Finally, although she struggled to keep it in, her words burst out with unpremeditated pain, 'The painting won't! It was the best one I've ever done, the one I was going to show you, for you to critique.' She dropped her head onto her folded arms, which rested on her knees.

Looking at her in startled amazement, his eyes moved from the just visible oozing cut on her head to the freely bleeding leg wound, which to him looked very nasty indeed, and finally to the painting lying pathetically on the ground beside her. It appeared, of the three, it was the damaged painting which distressed her the most. He had to add courage to everything else he liked about her. His ex-wife would have demanded that he should dial the emergency services, probably the air ambulance, and would no doubt have been screaming the place down. Come to that, Gina wouldn't have come anywhere near a place like this, anyway.

After a long pause, Daniel spoke with considerable concern. The look of her knee made his stomach turn, and he was sure if it wasn't painful now, it soon would be. 'Look, whatever you say about being all right, this has to have been a nasty shock for you. I'm going to take you back to the cottage and clean up that cut for you. Or better still, get someone professional to look at it,' he added dubiously. 'Here, give me your hand. I'll help you up.'

He leaned forward and stretched out his hand. Claire raised her eyes, still bright with tears. She looked utterly miserable, and he couldn't help comparing her to the laughing, animated woman of yesterday. His heart shifted in his chest.

Silently she held out her hand, grimy, bloodstained, and sore.

He helped her to her feet and bent to pick up her case and the picture. Carrying those in one hand, he slid his other arm round her waist.

He heard her swallow. Was aware she flinched. Wondered if she was thinking the same as he was—that to be so close might prove difficult? Yesterday—his thoughts kept sliding back to the sunshine, talk and laughter of yesterday—they'd laid the foundations of a friendly relationship, and while he knew he could manage that, he was a lot more uncertain of being physically close. One day, he thought wistfully. One day. But it would be too much emotion now—emotion he wasn't ready to cope with.

'Put your arm round me,' Daniel suggested, determinedly concentrating on the thought she needed his help.

She turned her head and looked at him. He could sense her resistance. Fuck! Surely, they'd got past this yesterday, and had both silently agreed to put it to one side. Fine decisions, as long as warm body didn't come into contact with warm body and arms didn't entwine.

'Put your arm round me,' he repeated, knowing his

awareness showed in his eyes and seeing an answering flare of colour sweep over her pale cheeks.

'No. No, I'm sure I can manage,' Claire said faintly. She stepped forward as she tried to evade his arm, stumbling as she did.

'Look, don't be so silly. All we need is for you to fall again. Believe me, you're shocked and distressed and you need help to get home. I happen,' he added desperately, 'to be the only person around at the moment so...' His mouth went dry and his heart pounded so hard he thought she would see his body shake with each beat. 'We have to do this, okay?' he finished weakly.

What he couldn't understand, in view of his decision to never love again, was where this tender care and visceral attraction came from?

Wrong time, though. It really was the wrong time.

He waited. Slowly, Claire lifted her arm and slid it round his waist. He could feel her warmth through the thin cotton of his shirt as her fingers passed over the hard muscles of his back. He heard her swallow a second time and knew she was finding it hard to touch him in this way. Looking at her averted head, seeing the thick curl of her hair over her shoulders, he bit on his lip, struggling to maintain his detachment, but it was no use, because there was another of those strange, frozen moments which wrapped them in its embrace, even though neither looked at the other. Oh, where the hell was that easy camaraderie they'd shared yesterday?

It was several seconds before Daniel could speak. 'All right?' he asked, taking a ragged breath. He turned his head turned away from her, his voice curiously muffled as they slowly set off.

'Mmm,' Claire murmured, apparently also incapable of coherent speech.

Her head slipped sideways and rested against his shoulder, and her arm tightened slightly round his waist. They could have been lovers, he thought wistfully.

But no, not lovers, he admonished himself, as inside his feelings warred. It was just as he'd told her—he was the only one around to pick up the pieces after her accident. If there'd been someone else there, he would've relinquished his place with insulting speed. Nothing had changed. Well, it had, because now he knew her better, he liked her and cared about her well-being. That was what he had to keep uppermost in his head.

Yet Daniel remained constantly aware of the feel of her flexing body under the length of his arm, and the soft warmth of her pressed against his side.

It wasn't an easy walk back to the cottage and took a long time. Arriving at the door, he dropped his arm and stepped away from Claire, who swayed and put her hand against the door frame to steady herself while he dug in the back pocket of his jeans, extricated the key, and kicked the door open with his foot.

'Come on, you,' he said, reaching out to her again.

'No... no, really. I can manage now,' Claire protested, her hands weakly warding him off as she stepped forwards. 'Daniel... thank you... Daniel…'

He saw her sway and her eyes close, and a second

shaft of fear went through him. Leaping forward, Daniel caught Claire as she crumpled to the ground. She was more badly hurt than she'd let on. He carried her inert body into the sitting room and laid her gently down on the settee.

She needed a doctor who could take proper care of that leg and decide how serious the head injury was. She was too important and her injuries too severe for him to take further responsibility, dithering as he was between desire and trust issues. For a moment, he stood and allowed himself the fleeting luxury of taking in the details of her face before making his way upstairs, where he snagged a duvet from the spare bedroom and returned, covering her with it. Then he googled the hotel, got the number for reception, and asked for a message to be passed to Jake or Emily, asking them to contact a doctor.

While waiting for someone to arrive, he went into the kitchen and filled a bowl with warm water. Returning, he knelt beside Claire and gently cleaned as much dirt as he could from her face, hands and knee, but he refrained from touching the wounds.

Within fifteen minutes, Emily turned up at the cottage, looking worried.

'The doctor's coming to check her over,' she reassured Daniel, looking down at the white-faced Claire tucked under the duvet. 'I'm only thankful you were nearby when she fell.' Emily glanced at her watch. 'It's horrendously early, but Dr Tranter's a good bloke and said no worries. Jake's out running, otherwise he'd be here as well. Tell me what happened?'

What had happened? Claire had fallen. Claire was hurt. And the way Daniel felt her pain—as deep and raw as the wound on her knee—meant he had fallen, too. Or was falling. Hard and fast, and he wasn't sure he could stop it. But he'd promised himself friendship, so he'd have to.

CHAPTER 10

CLAIRE CAME ROUND to find herself on the settee with Doctor Tranter taking her pulse. She'd known the doctor since she was small. She smiled at him weakly.

'That's better,' he said approvingly. He remained silent for a few seconds, then released her wrist and lifted his stethoscope to her chest.

'So,' he said, 'what have you been up to? What on earth were you doing?'

'Trying to get somewhere in too much of a hurry,' Claire answered wryly, 'and as a result, achieving nothing.'

'Mmm, well, I wouldn't say that.' Doctor Tranter leaned over the settee and gently probed the cut on her forehead. 'You've achieved some very spectacular damage. Let's have a look at your leg.'

Daniel had obviously given the doctor a comprehensive run-down on all her injuries. Silently, Claire hitched herself up and leaned back on the cushions before pushing down the duvet. She noticed abstractedly that someone, Daniel again, she assumed, had attempted to clean her up, and was probably responsible for the duvet, as well.

'Mmm, ouch,' the doctor murmured. He looked at her over his glasses. 'Pity you were wearing shorts. I can glue your head wound, but after I clean up your knee, I'm going to put a couple of stitches in it. I'll give you a local anaesthetic, but you'll not feel so happy later on. How long's the boyfriend staying?'

'He's not my boyfriend. He's just a friend,' Claire said reluctantly. 'He's the one staying here, and I'm up at the hostel. He's only here for the summer because he needed a place to stay. He brought me here because it was the closest, but as soon as you've sorted me out, I'll take myself up to the hostel.'

The doctor looked up from his bag. 'Mmm. He seemed upset when he met me at the door.'

'Upset?' Claire queried. Well, maybe. They'd got on well enough yesterday, and she knew from their walk back here earlier that despite the control he exerted over his emotions, he wasn't completely unmoved by her. Although now she understood he didn't want an involvement.

'Yes, my dear. Quite agitated. I assumed, wrongly it seems, that he was your boyfriend and would be here to look after you for the rest of the day. I wonder... perhaps it might be better if you went into hospital for the night? Those hostel rooms aren't suitable if you're alone. You need someone to monitor you for the rest of today and tonight, most of tomorrow as well.'

'Whatever for?' Claire felt confused, looking at the

doctor questioningly. She hated to be shut in, unable to get outside in the fresh air and take at least a small amount of exercise. 'I certainly don't need to go to hospital. I've only fallen over! How many times does that happen when you're a child? You don't get carted off to hospital just for that.'

There was a knock at the door.

'Yes?' Claire called distractedly, still trying to take in what the doctor had said.

Emily came into the sitting room. 'How are you feeling now?' she asked kindly.

'Perfectly all right,' Claire said heatedly. 'And there's no reason at all to go to hospital! I've only fallen over!'

'When you fall as a child, you're small and you bounce easily. The damage you do isn't very great because of the lightness of your body. Falling as an adult is more painful. You fall a greater distance because you're taller and you fall harder because your bodyweight is greater.' Doctor Tranter was writing on a prescription pad as he spoke. He laid down his pen and directed his firm gaze at Claire. 'If there was going to be someone with you, then yes, you could stay at the hostel, but I want to stitch your leg and you've knocked your head badly. And on top of all that, you fainted—'

'That wasn't anything to do with the accident! Most likely because I didn't have any breakfast.'

'You fainted, and maybe it was not having breakfast, but maybe it was shock,' the doctor replied firmly. 'I don't want to leave you left alone in case you faint again. You might have a mild concussion, and you won't feel any better by the time I've stitched this up.' He patted her leg. 'I've also got to give you a tetanus shot unless you can swear to me you *know* your shots are up to date? Especially now you're working in the gardens.'

'Umm...' Claire murmured vaguely.

'Quite!' Doctor Tranter exclaimed.

'But there's really no need... I've got my mobile and Jake and Emily are just across the courtyard and will pop in every now and again, won't you, Emily? Or I could come and stay with you?'

Out of the corner of her eye, Claire saw Daniel slip in and lean against the wall.

'Both would normally have been possible, but don't you remember? Jake and I are heading to Birmingham for the Hospitality Fair at the exhibition centre. We're setting off this morning, and not back until late Wednesday, so no, we can't look after you.' Emily looked concerned. 'Does she really need a night in hospital, Dr Tranter?'

'Not if there's someone around to monitor her. Just for twenty-four hours.'

'Oh, this is silly!' Claire said angrily, dropping her face to rest on her hand, ashamed of the weakness of her easy tears. 'How about mum and I stay in your flat, Emily? Or I could go to hers? Yes, of course. That's the answer. I can stay at mum's.'

'Your mum's coming with us. There are things we thought she'd be interested in, and she's worked so hard, getting such a wonderful staff together. It's a bit of a treat for her.' Emily shrugged and spread her hands in apparent apology.

'Claire,' the doctor said gently, 'I've explained why I'd

prefer it if there was someone to monitor you, and you're an intelligent woman. It's a risk I neither want to take for your sake, nor can take from a professional point of view. Now I may as well wait until we get to the hospital before I stitch you up. You can come in my car and—'

'Do I understand Claire has to go into hospital simply because there's no-one round to keep an eye on her?' Daniel interrupted in a cool voice.

The doctor nodded.

'And she doesn't want to?'

They both looked at Claire, who kept her face hidden and shook her head.

Daniel shrugged. 'She could stay here if that's what's needed,' he said slowly. 'The bedroom upstairs is empty, and it seems a fair repayment for Claire giving up her new house for me, even if only temporarily. It would actually make me feel better about it, if you want the truth.' He leaned one shoulder against the wall, his hands thrust into his jeans' pockets.

As he calmly offered to let her stay, she wondered how she could maintain the outward appearance of friendship when the more she got to know him, the more they talked together, the greater were her feelings? Could she keep those feelings to herself if they shared the house for a day or two? If she couldn't, she might shatter this new-found bond between them. Intuitively, she recognised Daniel could manage her as a friend, and she didn't want to push things too much and cause him to retreat.

So even as she accepted it was a crazy idea, Claire

raised her head, hope dawning in her eyes. 'Would you?' she asked softly. 'Would you really let me stay here? I'd be very grateful. There's no need for me to be fussed over, but if it's going to worry Doctor Tranter, then I'll have to do as he says.' Claire's eyes fixed pleadingly on Daniel.

The doctor snorted. 'Silly girl.'

Daniel pulled himself away from the wall, his hands coming out of his pockets. 'She can stay, then. If Emily will show me what's needed, I'll get a few things together from your hostel room, Claire. Back in half an hour at the most, okay? Hand on heart, I'll look after you carefully and you can head back to the hostel late tomorrow.'

'Hell, yes,' Claire muttered. 'I need to get to work.'

'Not in the garden doing anything physical. You can do some office work,' Emily said sharply. 'Plant orders, looking over the old plans, things like that. You hear me?'

Resigned, Claire nodded.

Daniel looked thoughtful. 'You said yesterday you'd show me the plans? Maybe not today, but something we could do tomorrow if you feel well enough?'

Claire brightened, a faint smile on her lips. 'Sounds like a great idea. Emily, can you show him where they are?'

'Indeed I will. Now do as you're told or else I'll have Jake and Annie cross with me!'

The door closed behind Daniel and Emily as Doctor Tranter looked at Claire, one eyebrow raised, a smile twitching at the corner of his mouth. 'Mmm, yes, well. I agree he gave little away just then, but he was very concerned before. Have you known him long?'

'No, I haven't known him at all long.' She winced as the doctor carefully inserted the anaesthetic in her leg. 'Anyway, we're just friends for the moment. That's enough for him, because I think he's had a bad time recently and needs time to sort things out. It's weird, but I kind of fell for him when I first saw him.'

'It can happen like that sometimes,' the doctor answered. 'No rhyme or reason, nothing to explain it. Nothing you can do. Let nature take its course.'

'Nothing else I can do,' Claire said wistfully, thinking of the moments they'd shared. The time they'd both first seen each other and how their eyes had met and held in an enthralled attraction which had affected them both. The kiss, begun in anger and finished in tenderness, from which he'd fled, denying the desire that flared between them. And this morning, their mutual reluctance to be close, which on her part was because she knew it would be hard to hide how she felt. On his part, she could only guess it was because he still wanted to avoid emotional entanglements.

'Let nature take its course,' the doctor repeated soothingly, a twinkle in his eyes. 'You're a beautiful young lady, Claire, and a kind and understanding one as well. He'd be a fool if he couldn't recognise what was under his nose.'

Claire blushed.

'Right, I'm going to let that anaesthetic work. I'll clean up your head and glue it together while we're waiting. It'll hurt,' he warned, slipping out of his jacket and rolling up his sleeves.

Daniel returned as the doctor was putting a dressing over the cut on her forehead. He slid silently into the room and took up the same position, leaning against the wall.

'Hello, young man,' Doctor Tranter smiled over his shoulder. 'Do you know the signs of concussion?'

'Dizziness, disorientation, sickness?'

'Throw in headaches, brain-fog and double vision. It doesn't matter if she sleeps, but if you could check on her a couple of times in the night, just see if she stirs, you know?'

Claire made a gesture of repudiation.

'That's okay. I'll do that.'

'And if she faints, do you know what to do?'

'Umm… legs higher than her head, or recovery position?'

'If she's totally out, the recovery position. If she's just dizzy, legs higher than her head. You'll do.' The doctor turned back and started work on her knee, gently cleaning and disinfecting the nasty cut before inserting some stitches.

'Not the best of sewing, but it'll hold it together. They'll dissolve. No need to come and see me to have them taken out.'

As he worked, Claire stared with grim determination out of the window until he straightened up, satisfied, a clean dressing covering the damage.

'That should do. Right, young man. Out now. She needs tetanus and antibiotic shots. I'll drop a prescription in at the chemist for painkillers and some more antibiotics, and no doubt they'll get it up to you by tonight.'

The doctor completed his injections and tidied away his things. Finally, he stood by the settee and looked down at her. 'How are you feeling now?'

'Okay,' Claire smiled shakily.

'Liar. But then you always were a plucky little girl, trying to keep up with young Jake. Take it easy today,' he advised, 'and take some painkillers. That leg will hurt and your head will ache if it isn't already, okay? Have you got any to be going on with until the prescription arrives? I've put some on it as well as the antibiotics.'

'I'm sure Emily will have sent some down,' Claire said vaguely. 'Thank you, Doctor Tranter. I'm really grateful to you.'

She lay back on the cushions and her eyes closed. The doctor pulled the duvet up gently round her shoulders before quietly leaving the room.

Claire certainly didn't feel well. She was cross with herself for her carelessness in running along a path she knew had all kinds of pitfalls—rocks, loose sand, and gravel. She felt guilty about the unintentional time off she was being forced to take from work when she'd only been in the job for two or three weeks. And her family… somehow, she felt like they were deserting her, although of course she'd known about the exhibition. She was being completely illogical. She was more than fine here with Daniel until tomorrow evening at least.

The rest of today and most of tomorrow. A few tears of self-pity crept out from under her closed eyes and trickled down to catch on her lip, where she caught them on her tongue and tasted their weak saltiness. Would Daniel be friendly and relaxed like he'd been yesterday, or would he be withdrawn and suspicious of her motives again? Maybe under normal circumstances she'd like to add in something physical to their tentative friendship, but that was something she'd need to keep in the background. As long as he was friendly. Yes, as long as he was friendly, then she'd probably cope.

CHAPTER 11

Daniel was in the kitchen, competently preparing a sauce for the packet of dried pasta that lay on the work surface next to the cooker. The smell of tomato and garlic was fragrant and appetising.

Doctor Tranter stood in the doorway and watched in silence for a few moments as Daniel finished chopping some herbs, which he then added to the pan.

'Thanks for agreeing to let her stay here,' the doctor said quietly when Daniel had finished his task.

Daniel looked up. 'It's the least I can do, given the circumstances.'

'Perhaps.' The doctor was noncommittal, although his was gaze questioning as he stepped forwards. 'Mmm, smells good. May I try a bit?'

Daniel silently passed over a clean spoon, and Dr Tranter took a small sample from the pan, blowing on it to cool it down before tasting.

'Delicious. Anyway, back to you letting Claire stay… I'll repeat my thanks. It's good of you to do it.'

'Yeah, okay. As I said, she's given up her cottage for me, and if she dislikes hospital so much, it won't hurt me to have her here.'

Brave words. Daniel only hoped he wouldn't regret them. While his mind was clear about not wanting an entanglement, he wasn't sure his body would comply. He'd enjoyed being with Claire and the rest of her family yesterday and only hoped the two of them could continue to get on as friends while she was here. Anyway, there was a lot more to find out about her, and the garden plans to look at. Everything would be okay. It would. He was sure of it.

Full of determination, Daniel raked a hand through his thick, wind-tossed hair and leaned back against the work surface, arms folded across his chest. 'I promise I'll look after Claire while she's unwell, and then tomorrow she can probably return to the hostel, right?'

'Yes, she should be well enough by then to be on her own.'

'Okay. Consider it done.' Nothing much could happen in that time.

A silence fell in the kitchen, broken only by the soft simmering of the pan and the cry of the seagulls wheeling in the cloud-flecked sky beyond the window.

The doctor moved to the door. 'Well, everything should be fine, but if you're worried, phone the surgery. I'll call in again tomorrow. Probably around four, for a last check before clearing her to go home. Will you be around?'

'I will. Goodbye, Doctor Tranter.' Daniel held the door open for him and watched as the doctor walked away, and with a brief wave, disappeared round the corner.

Slowly closing the door, he went back into the kitchen and leaned on the counter. And now? He shrugged. It was easy. He ministered to Claire in her hour of need, enjoyed getting to know her a bit better as a friend, and then, as he'd told the doctor, she returned to her hostel room, and he remained heart-whole and unscathed.

Why, then, did he feel so uncertain?

During the morning, Daniel looked in on Claire three times, and each time she was sleeping, silky lashes fanned onto her flushed cheeks, hair tumbled on the cushions, the dressing on her forehead sharply white against her creamy skin.

Daniel leaned over the settee and whispered her name, and each time she stirred, a slight smile touching her full mouth, her fingers moving in response to his voice.

The third time he visited, he took her slim fingers in his own strong, brown ones, stroking his thumb across the back of her hand. A deep tenderness filled him, almost like a pain, even as his mind protested at his actions. Her fingers tightened trustingly round his and pulled his hand against her cheek. He felt the warm softness of her skin against his and left his hand where it was. She seemed so vulnerable, lying there. It soothed his aching heart to give way to the tenderness just for a moment, even as he wished it could be all the time.

Hardly daring to move, he stood for some moments, imagining what it might be like to be her lover, feeling his body stirring to passion under him. He bent and softly brushed his lips across her forehead. One day. One day when he'd got over all his shit, maybe he could come back.

A soft exclamation of distress broke from him, and he pulled his hand gently away, turning from the bed and striding to the door. He might be tired of his self-imposed refusal to get involved emotionally again, but it was for the best. At least it spared him the possibility of further hurt, and definitely spared Claire.

A sound made him turn. Claire was looking at him, eyes wide. He halted his precipitous exit and walked reluctantly back to the bed, willing the pounding of his heart to slow, pushing his trembling hands into the pockets of his jeans, hoping his slight erection would rapidly die down.

'How are you feeling?' he asked, careful to keep his face blank, hoping she'd been unaware of his gentle caress.

'All right, thank you. What's the time?'

'Gone two. Are you hungry?'

'Oh, yes!' Claire sat up, then winced, raising a hand to her forehead, eyes momentarily closing.

Taking a step forward, Daniel worried she might faint again, or some other problem might crop up, although the doctor had seemed happy enough to leave her in his care. To him, she looked far too pale, and he half-turned, thinking it would do no harm to ring the surgery to check.

While he was dithering, feeling anxious, her eyes reopened. 'I didn't have breakfast, remember?' Her face shadowed, and he knew she was thinking about her fall.

The tension seeped from his body and his stomach calmed. The relief was considerable. He would've hated for her to get worse. Food. Of course, that was why she looked pale. 'I'll bring you a sandwich. I've made some pasta for tonight so I don't want you spoiling your appetite.' Daniel's voice was even, and a slight smile touched his mouth.

Claire looked at him, but he couldn't make out her expression. Maybe cautious? Understandable, with them having to share the cottage for a couple of days. He felt cautious, too.

Abruptly, she dropped her eyes and threw back the duvet. 'I don't need you to bring me anything,' Claire announced. 'I'm getting up.'

She swung her feet to the floor and stood up just as Daniel moved closer.

'Wait!' he exclaimed. 'Take it slowly.'

'Ohhh!' Claire staggered under the onslaught of what appeared to be a wave of dizziness.

She put out a hand blindly, feeling for the settee, and fell against Daniel, who curved his arms protectively round her. For a moment he stood immobile, allowing her body, pliant and warm, to rest against his, her hair sweet to smell. Before he realised what he was doing, his lips touched her forehead with a featherlight kiss, barely discernible.

Fuck! A disconcerting mix of past and present feelings—bitterness and rage paired with tender hope and blooming attraction—swirled wildly through him.

If his legs didn't buckle under the pressure, his chest might cave in. Hate women or love Claire? He fought to draw in a steadying breath.

With a terrific effort of will, he pulled away from her and dropped his hands. 'Sorry... I'm sorry,' he muttered. 'Are you okay now?'

His arms felt strangely empty as they fell to his sides.

'Yes, yes, I'm all right.' She moved forward carefully. 'See? I'm doing well.'

They went outside onto the patio with its sweeping view across the bay, and Daniel brought out the sandwiches he'd made for her.

'I ate earlier,' he said. 'I've been sketching.' He gestured to the wall encircling the patio and Claire noticed for the first time a large pad of paper and some pastels resting on the stones. She walked over to look at his work.

In a few perfect strokes, he'd captured the impression, the essence, of the bay, inferring the sun dancing on the waves, the ruggedness of the rock contrasted with the smooth, wet sands, and the movement of gulls and fleeting clouds in the sky.

Claire drew in her breath sharply as she stood in silent contemplation.

After a few moments, Daniel stood and took a step towards her. 'Claire?'

She spun to face him.

'I'm sorry... I didn't mean to startle you, but you went rather quiet?'

'Your painting...' she gestured to the piece of work so carelessly flung down on the wall top, done in a sketchbook, never intended to be a formal piece. 'I realise now... I understand what level my talent is. You saw my painting this morning,' she finished sadly, dropping into a chair and staring sightlessly out across the sea. 'It was my best, I think.'

He was silent for a long time, sitting on the wall with his back to the magnificent view he'd caught so carelessly on paper. Finally, he sighed and stood, coming to join her in another of the chairs set round the small patio table.

'Your painting wasn't too bad.' He paused awkwardly. 'Many people would envy you your skills, and you'll always find a market for your work. That's quite an achievement. There aren't many artists who make the big time, you know. Most are on your level.'

'Thanks. Just as well it's only a hobby.' Claire shrugged then chose one of the sandwiches, biting into it with evident hunger.

'Emily stopped off at the kitchen gardens and we picked up the Victorian plans. I'd love it if we could look this afternoon and you could talk me through what you hope to achieve.'

'Ha! Might take this afternoon and the rest of the week.'

'I'm interested,' Daniel responded mildly. 'But I'm no expert, so keep it to words of two syllables, okay?'

Claire gave a half smile and picked up another sandwich.

Good. If she had an appetite, she was well on the road to recovery.

'You mentioned America a couple of times. What are you going for?'

'Oh, it's been arranged for some time. I'm doing some teaching, some demos, and going on a coastal painting trip with some American artists at the end of the academic year. I leave in September, and I'll be back at the end of August the following year.'

'Whoa! Some trip.'

'It should be interesting,' Daniel conceded, a slight smile on his lips. 'And I certainly feel very honoured they've asked.'

'Do you plan to come home in-between terms?'

He shook his head. 'They've booked me up with all sorts of things, so no. No time.'

Claire looked thoughtful, then she shook her head and smiled at him brightly. 'The plans,' she said. 'But before we do, I'd like to go for a bit of a walk. I feel stiff and if I move, I should loosen up.'

'Do you think you ought?' While he understood her need to move, her injuries were so new. What if they reopened? What if she fainted again?

'I'll only go as far as the rock.' She pointed to the large rock not that far away, a magnet for all the children, a challenge for them to climb. 'You'll be able to watch me to make sure I'm okay.'

'Your day-dreaming rock?'

She stared at him, a smile curling her lips. 'You remembered!'

'Well, it was rather pertinent to the discussion at the time, lending me your beloved cottage.'

'Indeed it was,' she murmured thoughtfully, and then

without waiting for his leave, she crossed the flagstones and went out of the gate. Watching as she walked over the firm sand and leaned on the rock, gazing out at the sea, he noticed the droop to her shoulders and guessed she wasn't as well as she'd have him believe. Maybe they better postpone those plans until tomorrow?

It amazed him she'd still not mentioned her injuries, had not claimed the accident caused her any distress. No doubt she would, eventually, though. Most women would, under the circumstances. It was too good an opportunity for her to gain his sympathy. His lips twisted, and he picked up his pad, only to be confounded minutes later when he realised he'd sketched her figure into his landscape, somehow capturing a lonely desolation to her pose with a sympathy he didn't know he still possessed.

Daniel stared at her, his pencil stilled. Claire would be easy to love. He already felt an unwilling sexual attraction, but there was more than that. He admired her for changing careers, and her calm sweetness of character, and the way she'd just accepted her injuries. Shaking his head, he sighed. This wasn't the route he wanted to follow. He had to step back. He wasn't ready.

The pencil and pad fell unheeded as he stood, raking a hand through his hair. Wasn't ready, or wouldn't allow himself to be ready? The thought sent shockwaves through him.

He watched her as she began the short walk back.

'See? Safely back.'

Daniel gave a half-smile. 'Good. Feel better for moving?'

'Yeah, I think so.'

'Do you feel up to looking at the plans or shall we leave it until tomorrow? Depends on your energy levels.'

'I'm good, honestly. Better for some lunch and the walk. Where did you put them?'

'In the sitting-room. Will we be all right out here?'

'Not much wind. Should be fine. Tell you what—you make some coffee, and I'll get the plans.'

Within ten minutes they were poring over the old Victorian plans as Claire enthusiastically explained what was still in place and what would need restoring.

'It's going to take you years,' Daniel sat back and looked at her admiringly.

The time had flown as they'd talked and pointed and he'd asked questions, and the enormity of the restoration had finally sunk in.

'Yes, but there's all the day-to-day gardening to do as well, and it would be great if we could get some vegetables growing. I've already planted a few late crops, but hopefully next year I can do a lot more. Certainly, there's plenty to do. I'll advertise for a second gardener once I'm more confident of how I want to move forward, and we might still need the contractors as well.'

'Contractors?'

'For lawn mowing, hedge cutting—stuff like that. Come on, that's way enough about me and my plans, though. You told me a bit about your painting methods yesterday, but there's more I want to know. Like is it enough for you as a career? It must be incredible, just painting all the time.'

Daniel's eyes sought the rock where, minutes before, he'd watched Claire and sketched her into his picture before he looked back at her, a grin on his face. 'Pretty incredible just being out in the garden all the time, too, wouldn't you say?'

Returning his smile, Claire nodded. 'Yeah, okay. Touché.'

'I suppose I'm lucky,' he admitted. 'I love painting and the freedom it gives me, and there's no need for me to agonise which direction to take. It's there, clearly in front of me, driving me. It's almost a compulsion, but I love it.' He was silent for a while before restlessly getting to his feet and pacing to the wall, picking up his sketchbook, the delicate pastel glowing in the afternoon sun like a jewel. 'You know yourself how you find a subject and decide which angle you want to approach it from, which medium you want to use—'

'I only ever use watercolours.'

Daniel smiled and placed the sketchpad on top of the file of plans for the garden. 'Fair enough. I use different ones and sometimes I'll do the same painting in oils, then pastel. Some scenes give you no choice— they know what medium they want to be painted in, but others give you more freedom.'

A companionable silence fell. Daniel watched Claire as she drank in the scenery, wincing on her behalf when she absentmindedly touched the dressing on her head.

'Tell me more about yourself,' he suggested abruptly. 'I know what your brother did, and does now. I even know about Emily, but I know nothing about you other than your passion for gardening. Do you like music? What kind? What books do you read? Are you interested in travelling?'

He wanted to know what she liked to do, where she enjoyed going, everything.

'That's a tall order,' Claire said with a laugh. 'To tell you everything. Still,' she shrugged, 'we haven't much else to do now we've looked at the plans.'

They talked easily for the rest of the afternoon, then they ate the pasta Daniel had prepared, staying out on the patio and enjoying the pleasant evening, watching the sun sink below the distant horizon, leaving a glittering trail of fire across the gently shifting waves.

'It's amazing,' Claire said idly, eyes narrowed against the red and gold path. 'This sea.... it never ceases to fascinate me. Like this, so tame, so beautiful. But in winter, it can be awful down here. I don't know what it will be like in Gardener's Cottage then.'

'Mmm. I'd wondered about that.' He gestured to where the tide lapped gently at the rocks immediately below them. 'It's a wonderful setting, though.' He inhaled deeply. Wine. Warm salt air. Seaweed. Her perfume.

'I know. I love this place.'

They both fell silent, letting the tranquil sound of the shushing waves lull them. Somehow, with the sea and the glorious sunset, it was easy to forget past pain, allowing softer feelings to creep in, feelings which subtly entrenched themselves into his heart. Was this the healing the counsellor had talked about? He'd warned Daniel he wouldn't wake up one morning and suddenly be over it, but it would be a gradual process. A happy moment here, appreciating a woman's company there. Such moments would increase over time until Gina was a mere shadow in his past. That, Daniel could accept, but he wasn't sure he'd ever forget his baby, though.

During the evening, they'd found they shared interests in certain books and music, but about personal matters Daniel remained silent. When Claire tried to find out about his emotional commitments, his face had darkened and he'd changed the subject sharply. Wisely, she'd taken the hint and steered the conversation back to safer topics.

'Well,' Claire eventually said with false brightness, draining the last of her wine, 'I think I'll go to bed now.' She gave him a small smile and turned, disappearing through the door without waiting for a reply.

She took the warmth of the day with her, the light too, leaving him alone and unhappy.

He should feel relieved she'd left, taking the danger of her presence with her, but he felt disappointed. It was an abrupt end to their lovely evening. His encounters with Claire had challenged his determination to remain unattached. She was steadfast, eternally kind, sweet, loving. His list could probably continue. But he still feared the next step, which meant trusting again. Eyes clouded with doubt, he remained on the patio for a long time, gazing across the swiftly darkening sky, regretting the impulse that had caused him to agree to let her stay with him. He'd known at the time it would be a dangerous thing to do, and the day's events had proved him right. All he could think of was that upstairs, someone he now liked and admired lay in bed, and it would be interesting to take things further. His thoughts were enough to make his body restless and his jeans unpleasantly tight. Too damned long without fucking a woman. It was no wonder she was making his lust rise. Not a lot he could do about it, though. Oh, hell! This mental merry-go-round was exhausting.

He checked on Claire before eventually retiring to bed, where he slept fitfully, disturbed by erotic dreams which centred round the bright loveliness of her. He woke around three in the morning, finding himself still hard and ill at ease. He sat up and ran his fingers through his hair in exasperation. Normally he might have relieved his sexual tension, but it seemed distasteful, with Claire lying only feet away, even if she was on the other side of a wall.

What would happen if he went into her bedroom, suggested they made love?

Surely, he'd learned his lesson? Surely, he'd been hurt enough not to be foolish and risk all the pain again? Claire wasn't someone up for a one-night screw. She'd want more. Long term. He wasn't going to do long term ever again.

Striding to the window, Daniel pulled aside the curtain to look out at the shifting waters of the bay. His own feelings shifted, from resentment to longing for an end to this conflict. One thing was sure, he wouldn't get to sleep again. It was nearly time to check on Claire, anyway. He'd set his alarm for four o'clock.

Pulling on jeans, he drifted downstairs and made himself some coffee before moving outside onto the patio to drink it. The night was cool and still, the sky completely clear and the full moon of the last night or two now looked noticeably lop-sided as it waned. It was still enough to cast a bright light over the scene, causing sharp shadows where the rocks stood on the sand. The tide was on the turn, and the gentle sound of the waves was soothing. He rested one foot on the low wall, leaning his forearm on his thigh as he gazed sightlessly over the incoming water.

There was only today to get through. Later, he could send Claire back up to the hotel because the doctor had said she'd be okay by then. He could manage today. He could paint for most of it. She wouldn't need him to stay close. He shook his head in exasperation, raising his mug, drinking deeply. Right. He would check on Claire, go back to bed and later on, he'd prepare a canvas on which to paint the bay scene sketched out yesterday. With Claire leaning on her rock.

He turned to go back inside before pausing, his head on one side, hearing something above the suck and flow of the waves on the beach. The window above his head was a casement, open to the night air.

The small bedroom. Claire's window. And she was crying.

Softly, he had to admit, and if he'd still been in his room, with the bathroom in between, he doubted he'd have heard her.

In seconds, he was outside her door. He knocked softly. 'Claire?'

A sudden silence fell within the room, broken by the occasional soft gulp of distress she couldn't suppress.

'*Claire?*'

She clearly realised he wasn't going away. 'Y-yes?'

'What's wrong? May I come in?'

'N-no. No. There's nothing wrong. You just woke me up, that's all. Thank you, Daniel, but go back to bed.'

Liar, he thought, but he turned with relief away from the door. Then, knowing he couldn't leave her, he turned back. She was hurting, and he had an overwhelming desire to comfort her. He pushed other thoughts to the back of his mind. She sounded in no state to have him try anything else, and nor, he realised in surprise, did he want to. He simply wanted to hold her until the tears stopped.

Other than the moonlight filtering in through the curtains, darkness shadowed the room. It gave enough light for him to see Claire, lying on her front, her face pressed into the pillow as she tried to smother the sound of her crying. He approached the bed silently on bare feet.

He touched her shoulder, and she jumped, twisted a face so miserable towards him he never hesitated. He dropped onto the bed and turned her round, gathering her to him as he'd longed to do since he'd found her, dusty and blood-stained, at his feet yesterday morning. Rocking her in his arms, warmth flowed through him, melting more of the ice around his heart as he sought to comfort her.

It felt right for the comforting to change to kisses on her eyes, her cheeks, her lips, and his caring hands to change, and become instead seeking hands that stroked and caressed her.

If she'd recoiled, pushed him away, turned her face to the side, it wouldn't have surprised him, but the opposite happened, and her arms pulled him closer, returning his kisses with such feeling it surprised him, even as he allowed himself to be engulfed by her, swept along in a torrent that shook him to his core. Moving his hands on her face, he cupped her jaw, lightly stroking back the hair, tumbling round her shoulders.

Murmuring her name, Daniel rolled on top of her, his mouth seeking, his hands moving to touch her breasts, his erection pressing into her softness. She arched her body under his, her hands plucking in frustration at the denim of his jeans. Raising his head, his vision cloudy, he eased upright, kneeling over her, his hands replacing hers as he reached for his zip.

His actions slammed into his mind and his head jerked up, his eyes clearing, seeing everything in stark clarity. He froze. What the fuck was he trying to do?

CHAPTER 12

CLAIRE OPENED HER EYES, unable to bear the feel of cold air on her skin after the smooth warmth of Daniel's body and the musky smell of him surrounding her. He was kneeling above her and the sheer beauty of his broad chest, the arrow of dark hair on his belly, his long-fingered hands ready to unzip his jeans and release the clearly visible erection shot a bolt of pure lust through her as heat and moisture built inside.

But… he'd stopped and held himself motionless as he stared down at her, his eyes aware and horrified. What…?

With an inarticulate exclamation, he tore himself from the bed and stumbled to the door.

'Daniel!' The pain of his rejection wrenched a shocked wail from her.

He looked back once, his eyes dark pools of anguish in the fitful light of the moon, then the door closed behind him with a slam, leaving the room achingly empty except for the hurt of his humiliating rejection.

If Claire had felt distressed before, it was nothing to the pain searing through her now, but if Daniel heard her sobs this time, he made no move to come again to comfort her.

By six o'clock, Claire gave up on any pretence of sleep. She's spent the last two hours wondering why, when it was so clear he had feelings for her, he'd denied them again. She could understand he'd had a bad time somewhere down the line, probably recently, but surely that's what happened to everyone at some point, and they all got over it and moved on.

Didn't they?

As she dragged a brush through her hair, her white face and shadowed eyes appalled her, and she wondered how she could face Daniel this morning. Had she been too pushy when he'd kissed her? He may have been the one to come to her room, but it'd only been because he'd heard her crying. Crying because of tiredness, an aching head, the aftermath of three years of intense work and her job change, moving, meeting Daniel, shock—any or all of those reasons could be the cause. Then, after he'd been so caring all day, more crying because he wouldn't let himself trust her.

But s*he* was the one who'd blatantly encouraged him when she'd first noticed his butterfly kisses. If she'd held back, told him no, then at least today they could face each other with dignity. As it was, she was afraid Daniel would be angry with her, and the easy footing of the day before would have gone, their tentative friendship lost.

Noticing the door to his room was ajar, she peeked

in. He'd made the bed, and it was very tidy. Colour swept over her face as she remembered the feel of his erection under her seeking hands and how she'd shamelessly pulled at his jeans, frustrated by the barrier of cloth between their bodies.

Slowly, she walked down the stairs, a frown on her normally smooth brow. Her head still ached slightly, and her knee was stiff and sore. Definitely time for some of those painkillers the pharmacy had dropped round yesterday afternoon.

But first, she wanted to locate Daniel. Clear the air. Try to make things right between them, because she'd enjoyed Sunday and yesterday so very much.

He wasn't in the sitting room. Wasn't in the kitchen.

In a sudden panic, Claire pulled open the French windows and ran onto the patio, scanning the deserted beach. No-one. There wasn't a figure in sight anywhere. Then... where was he?

Blindly sinking down onto a chair, Claire stared at the sea, dismay sinking into her stomach like a cold lump of ice.

He'd gone out somewhere. Of course he had. She should have realised Daniel wasn't the type to hang around and try to be polite in the face of what had happened. He'd made it clear he wanted no involvement and yet somehow, he'd let down his guard and allowed the feelings he felt for her to surface. She could guess, oh, yes, she could guess at his anger and his confusion this morning.

She knew he'd walk away from what had happened. The distant look would return to his face as he deliberately turned his back on the warmth and laughter they could have shared, not just as friends but, oh, as lovers as well.

Claire raised a clenched fist to her mouth and bit hard on her knuckles, the sea blurring in front of her eyes. How could Daniel be so *stupid*? Surely last night had meant something to him? She *knew* it'd meant something to him. She'd felt his body melt into passionate warmth in her arms.

He'd told her he used women, so why hadn't he used her last night? Why had he held back? What the hell had happened to him to make him like this, anyway, so… so *wounded*?

Claire finally stood, gathering a semblance of dignity about her. After a quick breakfast and swallowing two of the prescribed painkillers, she passed the day working. Settling on the settee, she looked through the plans for the garden, making copious notes, and found the nearest local nursery on the internet, finally ordering some bulbs and other plants from a wholesaler. To finish, she drew up some plans for the kitchen garden and was satisfied she'd done her best to earn her wages, fall or no fall. But despite occupying herself with her garden tasks, she couldn't stop thinking about Daniel. Especially the bombshell he'd dropped about going to America for nearly an entire year. That rather put an end to any future she might have envisaged. Sighing, she stared off into the distance. It really would be best if she let this whole thing go.

The doctor came at three in the afternoon, raising his eyebrows to find her alone. He accepted Claire's halting explanation that Daniel had gone for a walk and passed her as fit.

'Although by fit, I don't mean go mad, young lady!' he eyed her sternly. 'That was some fall and I really think you should take it steady for a day or two.'

'Okay.' Claire shrugged. 'I'm taking my tablets and I can say hand on heart I've spent most of the day sitting down.'

'Good. I don't need to see you again. But make sure you contact the surgery if you're worried. Any headaches or dizziness, signs of infection. Although there shouldn't be. Take care, Claire, okay?'

Claire made a sudden decision. 'Hang on. Can you spare five minutes while I get my stuff? Then give me a lift back to the hostel? Jake and Emily will be back tomorrow, and if you say I'm okay, there's no need to impose on Daniel any longer.'

Dr Tranter glanced at his watch, then back at her. He was silent for a moment, one eyebrow raised, before he gave a brief nod. 'Like that, is it? Okay, but only five minutes, mind.'

Settled back into her hostel room, Claire instantly felt restless and miserable. Stupidly, having just arrived back at the hotel, she now craved a walk on the beach. She could take a buggy down, slip past the cottage and get onto the shore by the hotel gate. Safe enough because she knew Daniel was out.

The day had been another sunny one and now the sun was slipping down in the western sky, spreading a wide pathway across the sea, casting stark shadows of the rocks over the beach. She was blind to the beauties of the evening, but welcomed the stretch of her muscles as she walked mechanically along. Her head was bent, her heart sore, as she tried to work out the enigma of Daniel Morgan, who could kiss her with such sweetness and then recoil from her with such insulting speed.

Why couldn't he let himself try again? Why didn't he—

Her spiralling thoughts were abruptly interrupted as she tripped over a small rock half buried in the sand and stumbled forwards into a tidal pool. She slithered about at the edge of the water, her feet fighting for a grip on the sliding sand, before realising there was a solitary figure rapidly approaching. Glancing up, she realised it was Daniel, and her heart sank as she observed the warring emotions of concern, irritation and dismay playing over his features.

Well, she could match those, every single one of them, and why was it him who turned up every time she made a complete idiot of herself?

'Don't just stand there!' Claire exploded. 'I need a hand to get out of here! It's sloping down and I'm sliding in! I'll get my leg wet.'

Moving forward, Daniel held out his hand. Gripping hers, he pulled her firmly away from the edge of the pool, where she stood looking down at her dripping ankles and the water running from her canvas shoes.

A quick glance upwards showed a faint smile unwillingly tugging at the corner of his mouth, and the corners of his eyes crinkling in amusement. Oh, how such humour suited him. Far better than his cool detachment.

As he noticed her gaze, she saw the smile disappear, and he turned to walk in the direction of the cottage, speaking over his shoulder as he left. 'You seem to be accident prone.'

'No,' Claire replied, taking refuge in an arctic voice, the hurt of his rejection last night bolstering her. Whirling, she ran after him and caught him by the arm. 'I'm no more accident prone than most. *You* seem inclined to follow me about!'

He stopped, a frown darkening his face. 'Whoa! I'm not following you. I was walking this way first and went as far as the sea-cave before turning back for home. I saw someone coming along the beach towards me, but you were silhouetted against the sun, so I didn't realise it was you until you fell in the pool.'

'Well, okay,' Claire commented, her irritation subsiding. 'I suppose there's not much point in continuing my walk now. I'd better go back and change.'

An uncomfortable silence fell as both of them remembered Daniel's clearly stated intention he was returning to the cottage. He could hardly walk off and leave her. Equally, Claire didn't want to force herself on him in view of what had happened last night.

'I'll wait,' Claire began, just as Daniel said, 'Go on if you like, I'm in no hurry and—'

They both stopped, their eyes locking together as a thousand messages seemed to fly between them.

Claire swallowed and turned to face the way she'd come. She knew she could forgive him for disappearing because she recognised the reason for it. She hoped one day to wear down his resistance and discover what that reason was.

'Let's not be silly. Surely we can walk back together amicably?'

Daniel hesitated for a long moment before nodding reluctantly and falling into step beside her.

They walked in silence, Claire unsure how to restore communication without showing how upset she was about the episode during the early hours of the morning. She felt she'd behaved badly by encouraging him. The very thing she'd warned herself against doing. No pressure, friends only. Pity it was so damned hard.

At last, Daniel cleared his throat. 'How are you feeling?' he asked gruffly.

'Me?' She was startled, immediately wary. 'I'm fine, thanks. There's no reason I shouldn't be, is there?' Her voice took on a defensive note, thinking he might be referring to last night. A flush crept across her face. Seconds more and they would have —

'Your head...' Daniel said hastily, interrupting her thoughts. It was obvious he, too, had realised his initial enquiry was open to misinterpretation. 'Your leg...' He gestured downwards with his long-fingered hand.

'Thank you, but they're both fine. I had a slight headache earlier, but it's gone now. The knee's stiff, but as you can see, I'm walking okay.'

'It's a beautiful evening,' he said inanely.

They walked a few more steps as she sought for a neutral topic. 'Daniel, do you have family? Siblings, and stuff, I mean,' she added hastily.

There was a silence. She looked at him to see him

frowning, looking down at their moving feet. Oh, hell… was this more stuff to do with his determination to keep women at arm's length? She really should learn to keep off personal stuff.

Finally, his voice low, he answered. 'My mother lives abroad with someone. I've lost track of who because she gets through them so fast. My father eventually remarried, and they both live in Provence. No siblings, though.'

Claire seized on the word Provence. That was surely neutral enough. 'Sounds good. I love Provence. I've only been twice, but I'm a Van Gogh fan and wanted to visit Arles then went to the Quai D'Orsay museum in Paris to see his paintings. Do you know, I was so disappointed in the starry night one there? Only because I thought it would be much bigger.'

He gave a brief laugh. 'Yes, it's a bit of a let-down, isn't it? The size, I mean. It's so vibrant you expect an enormous canvas. The St Remy one in New York isn't much bigger, either. He was a wonderful artist, though.'

They wandered slowly along the beach, talking about Van Gogh and his sad life, Claire telling Daniel about her trip and how she'd loved the Alpilles. Apparently, his father didn't live far from the strangely shaped mountains and he, too, appreciated them.

They reached the steps up to the cottage. Claire hesitated, wondering if talking about what had happened between them in the early hours of the morning was a good idea now, or not, but then decided to bring it into the open, and apologise. It would clear the air and break the slightly stilted atmosphere between them.

'Last night... Daniel, I'm sorry. I know events sort of caught us both by surprise, but I'm very aware I behaved rather badly and was encouraging you into things I know you're uncomfortable with. I understand why you left, and it was the right thing to do, it really was. Can we let it go? Please?'

She saw his startled glance, heard him release his breath as tension seep from his shoulders, his hands leaving the protection of his pockets.

'I should say sorry, as well. I came in to check on you, and you looked so lovely...' Looking embarrassed he gave her another quick glance. 'I can't give you what you want, but can't we still be friends? I enjoyed yesterday and the day before. We get on. We enjoy a lot of the same things, don't we?'

'Friends. Oh, yes, *I* could do that.' Claire fell silent before plucking up the courage to continue. 'But friends tell each other their pain, talk things through. You won't open up at all—it was me who brought this up to clear the air, while you would have said nothing, let it fester and retreated to being defensive. *I've* accepted we can be friends, but now I think that's something you need to work on.'

She saw his look of dismay before she turned to leave, quietly slipping away into the gathering gloom of the night. She'd said enough.

Claire avoided meeting Daniel over the next few days. She couldn't take any more hurt and enjoyed the peaceful solitude of the gardens. The discovery of old beds in the kitchen garden excited her as she set to work restoring them. She also arranged for someone to dismantle and remove the old greenhouses and replace them with just one, although it was going to be quite large.

As she worked, she veered between hope and despair. Someone had to make the first move to restore their friendship, and she'd had an idea.

She owned a book about Van Gogh, which she wondered whether he might be interested in. Come Friday evening, she'd pop down and offer it to him. Hopefully, he'd offer her coffee and they could talk. He needed her as a friend and seemed happy for her to fulfil that role. Over time, all she could hope for was surely something would grow from that?

CHAPTER 13

DANIEL SPENT his week walking to remote areas on the coast path to take photos and returning to the cottage to paint. He'd loved talking with Claire about art and her garden plans, and enjoyed walking with her on the beach. He seemed to find healing moments with her, and he wanted more. But not that kind of *more*. Why did they have to ruin that loveliness with the promises men and women didn't seem capable of keeping? He simply wanted friendship.

Even when he immersed himself in creating a painting, Claire intruded on his thoughts, and his frustration grew. It was frustration with his mind, which seemed to refuse to relax and let Gina's poison go, freeing him up to love again. It was also physical frustration. Especially physical frustration, after being so close to losing it the other night, and making love with Claire.

Perhaps if he sorted that out, he wouldn't be so

fixated on her and he could find some peace? Perhaps… he should have one of his casual flings, the ones he had resorted to in the last couple of years to ease his need for sex without the need to have a girlfriend. The women he took up with, just a handful, were ones he'd met in various places and who seemed as lonely and distant as he was, happy for a one-night stand and to walk away the next day with no promises or sweet words of love.

Scrolling through his contacts, Daniel found the name of a woman he'd spent the night with a few weeks before. She'd told him if he ever wanted to see her again, he'd be welcome, no strings attached. Shaking his head as he texted her, he wondered what *she* got out of her casual sex. They'd not talked much. Maybe she was like him and had a past which prevented her from commitment? She hadn't hinted she wanted a gift, or anything else, from him. If he asked her down here, offered to collect her from the nearest station, took her out to dinner and then spent a couple of nights screwing her, it might rid him of this overwhelming physical desire for Claire, which he was finding very difficult to deal with.

Louise texted back, full of enthusiasm for a weekend by the sea in his sweet little cottage. He felt the first stirrings of concern about his plan as he read her platitudes, unwillingly comparing them to Claire's plain-speaking. But it was done, and on the following Friday evening, he collected her, wined and dined her, and brought her back to Gardener's Cottage.

Even as he unlocked the door, his conscience twinged. He shouldn't be bringing her into what was Claire's home, even if she'd not properly moved in.

'Oh, Daniel, this is so, so sweet.' Louise moved ahead of him into the small sitting room with its whitewashed walls and exposed beams, her arms extended, a fixed smile on her face. 'But it's very lonely. Will we be safe?'

Crouching to switch on the electric flame fire, he turned his head to offer a perfunctory smile, feeling not the slightest bit of lust, and all the time, making comparisons. Her dyed hair to Claire's tumbled curls, her made-up face to Claire's beautiful and natural skin, her voluptuous figure to Claire's soft curves and lean strength. He huffed out a long breath and returned his gaze to the flames. What had seemed an excellent solution to at least one of his problems now seemed to have backfired. He'd wanted an uncomplicated fuck, so why did he feel he was cheating on Claire? He wasn't even sure he'd be able to manage an erection.

Wearily, he stood. 'Glad you like it.'

'Come here, lover boy,' Louise murmured, beckoning him with her red-painted nails. 'I had such a good time with you before, and I'm looking forward to tonight. Come here. Let's get started, why not?' She slid the strap of her dress down over her shoulder, exposing the top of one breast, licking her lips and swaying suggestively.

Staring at her consideringly, Daniel couldn't remember her being so overpowering previously, but that had been before Claire. Standing immobile, he allowed her to rustle up to him, his brain only capable of one thought—he was letting Claire down just as his mother and wife had let him down, and he didn't like it.

Louise slid her hands up his chest and undid his shirt. 'Come on. Put your arms round me. Show me some of the fire you had when we last met.' Her hand slipped inside to caress his nipples. Although they tightened at her touch, they caused no frisson, no echo of a response anywhere else in his body.

'It wasn't fire,' Daniel said flatly. 'It was a fuck, which we agreed at the time we both wanted. Feelings didn't come into it, but you seemed quite happy about it.'

She frowned. 'Well, look, I'll take whatever's on offer, okay? That's why you invited me, isn't it? To screw?'

I can't do this, I can't do this, I can't—

She cut off his thoughts by pressing her body against him, and pulling his head down before covering his mouth with hers.

But he couldn't respond. Not with his mouth, not with his hands, and not with his penis, which remained stubbornly soft. All he felt was shame and self-loathing. Too much of a coward to risk any kind of relationship with Claire, it seemed he was now condemned to no sex, because touching another woman felt like betraying her.

It was at that moment, horrifically, unbelievably, he heard her voice.

Claire's voice.

But it couldn't be. It couldn't possibly be. He'd conjured her up, surely?

Pulling back from Louise, he turned his head, his eyes widening in horror.

No figment of his imagination. She stood in the doorway, a book in her hand.

'I'm sorry,' she said coolly. 'I didn't know you were… *busy*.'

He could see her eyes. See her shock.

Disengaging himself from Louise's clutches, he stepped forward. 'Claire! It's not what it seems.'

The eternal cry of every man or woman found in a compromising situation which shattered the other person's trust.

Fuck, fuck, *fuck*!

He was pathetic. He was stupid. He was a coward.

Moving towards her, his hand stretched out, and a look of pleading on his face, he foolishly hoped to make her stay and listen.

Tell her not only had nothing happened, but he intended nothing would, either.

Oh, indeed a foolish hope.

Claire whirled and left, and when he followed her round the cottage, he watched helplessly as she drove the buggy at full speed towards the hotel.

Louise had followed him outside. 'And who was that?' she asked, acid lacing the saccharin sweetness of her voice.

'A friend. Just a friend,' he replied wearily.

Her eyes narrowed. 'Really? Seemed a bit more important to you than that.' Turning, she flounced inside, leaving Daniel staring up the slope.

If he went after Claire, she'd probably lock her door

to him. Oh, *fuck*! He dragged his hands through his hair, shoulders hunched. This wonderful idea of his to cool his body down by spending the weekend in bed with Louise had completely backfired.

Shame weighted his steps, turned his feet to stone. He could barely bring himself to return to the cottage. Claire's cottage. Where another woman waited for him. He was a bastard. He'd hurt Claire, and dug himself another new, and unwanted, hell to live in. And now he was going to upset Louise as well, because that new pack of condoms was going to remain unopened.

Louise's complaints started as soon as he walked through the door. Eyes narrowed, she lit a cigarette, she sat down on the chair by the fire, crossed her legs, and blew a stream of smoke. 'I haven't come all the way down here to this God-forsaken place if you've already got a number on the side, darling! It's not my scene to share with anyone. Care to explain?'

Daniel turned from the cloud of noxious smoke, feeling numb. How was it one woman could look magnificent in anger, while another just looked mean and spiteful?

'Louise, the house has a no smoking policy. Could you put it out, please?' He passed her a small dish.

Angrily, she ground out her cigarette. 'Explain what's going on, please.'

'I've said nothing to you which might lead you to think we're exclusive,' Daniel said tiredly, sinking into a chair and reaching for the glass of whisky he'd poured before Louise had insinuated herself into his arms. 'But anyway, she's a friend. No more, no less.'

Did he want Claire to be more? If it was her who was here, instead of Louise, would he want to continue? The other night he'd had the chance and backed off. Was he now wishing he hadn't?

Rubbing a hand wearily across his face, his heart ached. He'd seen the hurt on Claire's face when she'd witnessed him in that embrace, and he knew he'd been a bloody idiot to set this thing up with Louise. When they'd met before, she'd seemed as happy as him to have the comfort and release of sex with no strings attached. It was a mutual arrangement which hurt nobody and needed no promises.

Hurt nobody? It had hurt Claire, and it had hurt him, because now he realised he might have finally destroyed any chance of something special between them. Inadvertently, it hurt Louise, too, but he had the feeling she'd soon shrug it off.

But surely that was what he'd wanted?

Oh, fuck! He was exhausted with all the emotions warring inside him—trust, distrust, caring, rejecting, attraction, retreat—and trying to pick his way through them and round them.

Daniel became aware Louise was standing close beside him, her hand running over his hair and sliding onto his jaw. He recoiled. Sitting on the arm of his chair, she leaned down towards him, deliberately exposing her cleavage, her hand now caressing his chest through the already open shirt.

'All right, only a friend. She's gone now,' she murmured, her husky voice, 'and I'd like an early night, darling.'

'I'll show you your room.' Daniel jumped to his feet with rapidity. Relief flowed through him. At least he didn't have to go any further with this. Damage limitation which, somehow, he needed to let Claire know about.

Louise pouted and rose to her feet, standing in front of him, her body pressed lightly against his. '*My* room?'

He looked at her. The expressionless eyes, at odds with her words, had told him here was a woman who wanted no emotional involvement. He knew, because he saw that same expression every morning in his mirror. Now, though, instead of identifying with her, he felt sorry for her. Any desire he'd felt for her had vanished. Sex was not the answer.

He wanted to make love instead.

He wanted to make love with Claire.

But whatever happened with Claire, he knew he couldn't sleep with Louise as he'd planned. He turned away, ashamed of the reasons he'd invited her down.

'*Your* room,' he repeated with finality, and led the way upstairs.

Instead of bodily release, Daniel spent much of the night tossing and turning, wondering how to sort this mess out, determined to take Louise to the station first thing in the morning. His brain went round and round and he knew he was being stretched to breaking point.

If he could just talk to Claire, explain how he felt, and how he needed to sort himself out before he could come to her and offer himself without the baggage Gina had left him with. He needed more time to come to terms with the cruel loss of his baby as well.

Claire needed to know.
He had to find the courage to tell her.

CHAPTER 14

Claire paced the room. Ever since she'd run back to the hostel last night, anger and distress had ravaged her. How could Daniel turn his back on her for that *tawdry* blonde? Her fists tightened, and her stomach heaved as she pictured them in each other's arms, remembered Daniel's lipstick-smudged face. Her mind refused to contemplate what might have come next.

Oh, this was no good! She'd make herself ill like this. Marching round her room all last night, Claire had furiously sorted through all her stuff, tidying, slamming drawers back once they'd been done, because it gave her some much-needed control over her life. Now she needed family, and she knew Emily and Jake had returned at around four.

Crossing the yard, she slipped into the hotel through the kitchen and took the private lift to the attic floor.

'Hi, Claire!' Emily greeted her cheerfully. 'How are you feeling now? Your face still looks rough.'

The cut was hardly noticeable, but the bruising still

lingered on her forehead. 'It's okay. I hope you had a productive time at the hospitality show?'

'Not bad at all. Some ideas for themed nights which we might consider, and some good marketing strategies. Your mum loved the domestic side of things.' For a few moments, Emily chattered on about the trade show they'd been to, with Claire making suitable comments.

But her tone was lacklustre, and it wasn't long before Emily gave her a keen look as she leaned back against the sink. 'Hey,' she said sympathetically, 'you're a bit fed up, aren't you? Listen—Paul brought a delivery up for us as they're short of a driver, and he asked if you'd be going down to the pub later on. Why not go? He'll cheer you up.'

Paul. Yes. He'd showed more than once he'd like to take her out. Claire found him pleasant enough, but he'd never interested her as a potential partner. He was a long-standing friend, however, and she felt in need of some uncritical company tonight.

'I could do with it,' Claire said wanly, sitting at the kitchen table.

Emily looked at her shrewdly and turned her back, returning in seconds to place a mug in front of her. 'Here, get that down you,' she said. 'Cup of tea always works wonders. And how about a slice of Jake's chocolate cake?' She smiled as Claire's face lit up. 'Thought so.'

In minutes, she returned with another mug of tea, two plates with forks and slices of cake.

'Come on, what's the matter? It's not just your fall that's done this. Do you want to talk?'

Over the hot tea and divine chocolate cake, moist, gooey and moreish, Claire told her about Daniel and everything which had happened over the last week.

'Be fair,' Emily advised, when Claire's words finally petered out. 'He's said nothing to make you believe there's something special going on. From what you've just said, you're slowly learning to be friends. So he's free to bring someone down for whatever reason, sweetie. He's promised you nothing. In fact, from everything you've told me, he's been very careful to warn you he *isn't* looking for anything long-term or special.'

'I know, I know. And I should give up on wanting him to feel the way I do,' Claire admitted quietly, 'because I know he's been hurt. I don't know when he'll get over it, but is it so wrong to want to be there when he does? Yes, we're friends for now, and I hope he feels he can talk to me, and I know I should be happy with that.' Claire wiped a finger through a smear of the chocolate icing and licked it clean. 'It was the whole circumstances, I suppose. We'd quarrelled, and I'd thought of an easy way to get back to just being friends again, so when I walked in on them, it hurt. Although he's said nothing, I'm sure he likes me as more than a friend. I can sense it, and there are things he's said and he...' Claire stopped. She wasn't sure she wanted to share the kiss, and she certainly didn't want to share the scene in the bedroom when they'd both nearly lost control.

Although if she told Emily, it might make it more obvious why she felt so rejected.

'Why has he invited another woman here if you think he likes you?' Emily straightened her fork and folded her arms. 'Are you sure about that?'

'Yes, I'm sure.'

'So let me get this straight—he likes you but invites someone down for the weekend? And from what you said, it wasn't to discuss world affairs, now was it? It doesn't sound to me as if he's interested. I'm sorry, but it really doesn't.'

Claire looked helplessly at Emily. 'Sex? He said once he had no emotion to offer, and he used women just for sex. It doesn't shake my belief, though. He *is* interested.'

'Mmm.' Emily took their plates and mugs over to the sink, with its far-reaching view over the back fields beyond the walled kitchen garden, before moving back to the table, patting Claire on her shoulder as she went past. 'You'll only end up hurt.'

'Maybe.' Claire hesitated, then hastily continued. 'In all fairness, he's warned me off from the start and told me to stop pushing him. I've got a bit of a conscience about not doing as he asked, and I've tried to go the friendship route. That's no hardship because I really like him as a person, and we've a lot in common, but there's always that spark between us, which is hard to ignore, certainly on my part.'

Probably on his, too, she realised.

'It seems to me as if you're not paying enough attention to how badly he's been hurt?'

'Yes, but—'

'But you want to save him? Rescue him? Show him all's not lost and he can love again?' Emily shook her head. 'Jake said he and Daniel talked just after he arrived. Jake looked furious when he told me, but said he couldn't give any details because Daniel had spoken to him in confidence. Apparently, it was something this ex of his had done, and it was pretty awful. It didn't surprise Jake Daniel hadn't come to terms with it yet. So just be careful, right?'

'Okay. Yes, okay. I'll be careful. Daniel seems able to shut down on the physical side of things, but I wish I found it as easy.' She rubbed a hand over her eyes, her breath escaping in a long huff. 'Let's see where the friendship takes us.'

'It's in your hands. I trust you. Now look—why not go down to the pub this evening, and relax a bit? It's Saturday night. Jake and I might even drop in later. He's at the café today and tomorrow. Jenny's got family for the weekend. In fact, why don't you and I go to the café before it closes, and cadge dinner? Then we can all go for a drink. Well, you and Jake can. I better abstain. I know you've been hard at work—I'm awed by what you're achieving in the kitchen garden.'

'Thanks. I'm glad you're pleased. Hey, how are things in the baby department?'

'Great. Jake's planning the surfing lessons already.'

They both laughed.

'Oh, I keep meaning to tell you—the PA who used to work for me is coming down here to take over the admin and front desk during my maternity leave. She's called Sasha Fielding. She got another job after my company closed down, but she's always had a hankering to live by the seaside, so she's coming for six months. If she likes it, she'll stay. She's taking over the smallest of our holiday lets in the yard. And Jake and I are going to buy a couple more lets and start an agency. I can run that from here and take care of the sprog at the same time. Okay—settled. Come over at six-thirty, ready to relax a bit.'

In need of something to take her mind off Daniel, and even if Saturday was her day off, Claire spent it working in the kitchen garden. Emily had said she was in awe of what she'd done, and Claire had to admit to great pride as bed after bed reappeared from the years of weeds and lack of care. In many places, frost and time had broken more of the old terracotta edging than she'd expected, which was a disappointment. It would be expensive to replace, but a lovely idea. Maybe she could find somewhere selling reclaimed building stuff, but if not, she decided she'd need to run the idea past Emily before ordering new, because of the expense.

A shower, quick hair-dry, some clean jeans and a pretty top, and Claire was ready. She'd enjoy a meal with Jake and Emily, and the pub was as good a place as any to go.

Later that evening, in the pub lounge, Claire had to smile as she watched her kid brother show off Emily and her growing bump to people they'd known all their lives.

Just as she'd drained her half pint of bitter, the door of the pub swung open and Paul came in, together with two or three others from their group of friends. He spotted Claire straight away and came across.

'Claire.' He greeted her with warm possession, putting his hand on her arm and kissing her on the cheek. His blond hair gleamed in the subdued lighting of the bar, and as always, he appeared immaculate, never wearing jeans but always slightly smarter chinos teamed with a sports shirt in summer, and a long-sleeved shirt and Barbour body-warmer in winter. Claire knew he fancied himself a county type, which, having grown up with him in the tiny town of Solhaven, mildly amused her. She also realised he thought he'd come up in the world when he'd been appointed manager of the local supermarket. Yes, he was okay, but despite his proprietorial kiss, he'd never appealed to her.

'Hi, Paul,' Claire responded, wishing she could feel about him the way she felt about Daniel. It would make life so much easier.

Paul peered at her. 'Claire, your face. What did you do?'

Claire repeated the story of her fall, but as Paul exclaimed and started telling a story of some accident he'd had a couple of years ago, her mind drifted back to Daniel.

What had happened last night, she wondered, after she'd stalked off? Unable to prevent it, the scene she'd witnessed as she'd entered the sitting-room re-entered her mind. Daniel, his chest bared and gleaming in the lamp-light, lipstick on his well-cut mouth, that woman with her hair disarrayed, her eyes glittering with desire, dress half-off. *What had happened*? Had they sunk down onto the rug in front of the fire, or had they drifted up to *her* bedroom, the one she'd vacated so willingly for him? Could she ever go back to the cottage with those images burning in her mind?

Yet Emily was right. She'd no claim on him at all, so why did she feel betrayed? Friends shouldn't mind if one of them has the good luck to find someone… special.

'Claire?'

Startled, Claire brought her attention back to Paul, standing patiently beside her at the bar. 'I'm sorry?'

'I asked you if you'd like another drink?'

Claire dragged her attention back to Paul. 'I suppose,' she said. 'Thank you. I'm not… very good company tonight, I'm afraid.'

'Say that again,' he answered, his mouth pulled down at the corners. 'Anything to do with him?' He nodded his head toward the next room. 'You went off to sit with him the last time you were here, remember? And Jenny told me you were all having a good time together at the café last week. She called him your young man.'

Glancing over, her body filled with icy shock. There was Daniel. When had he come in? How had she missed him? Maybe he'd been there since she'd arrived? Leaning back, she could see the other chairs at the table. No-one was there. No blonde.

'Yes,' Claire admitted uncomfortably. It was better Paul knew the truth, then he might back off. 'I'm sorry, but yes. Although I'd hardly call him my young man. Jenny's ahead of herself there. He's a friend.'

'But you'd like more? Oh, well.' Paul's voice sounded mild as he turned to buy the drinks. 'We can all dream, I suppose.' But his mouth was thin with annoyance, and he flashed an unfriendly look in Daniel's direction. Claire sympathised—she knew just how he felt.

The group in the corner grew larger as the night progressed and various friends dropped in to socialise.

Something must have caught Daniel's attention, maybe the noise they were making, because finally he turned in Claire's direction. The crowd of people around her parted and their eyes met. Daniel paled and half-rose from his chair.

As quickly as he'd risen, he hesitated, shrugging almost imperceptibly, and allowed himself to drop back.

Claire slid off the stool, unable to bear it. It was clear, even though he was alone, he was going to ignore her. She didn't have to sit here, knowing he was shutting her out again. What had happened to their friendship, even if it had been short-lived so far?

'Paul, I have to go. Can you tell Emily or Jake I'm walking back?'

Paul searched her face and obviously saw something which worried him. 'I could give you a lift if you like?'

'Thanks, but you're drinking.' She looked at the half-finished pint in his hand, his third since arriving.

His cheeks flushing, he gulped some of the beer down, wiped his hand across his mouth, and gave a terse nod. 'Yeah, sorry. Point taken. Yes, I'll tell them. Be careful.'

The tide wouldn't allow her to walk along the beach, so she took to the cliff path. It wouldn't start getting dark until gone ten, and she'd be back long before then. She needed the walk. With each step and each thought crowding her mind, she imagined her finger jabbing him in the chest.

He was so stupid.

He knew by now they had something going for them.

There had been no need to invite that woman.

His rejection just now was thoughtless.

He was so... so... *blind*!

She wanted to slap some sense into him, but... but she couldn't. She couldn't even hold on to her anger. It ebbed away, as inevitable as the tide leaving the shore. She sighed, her steps slowing. He'd been hurt, his trust shattered, and he wasn't ready to heal.

Emily had warned not to push too much, and she wouldn't, but, oh—she shook her head—why the hell wouldn't he *talk* to her?

Oh, fuck him! Nothing to be done, except try to get over him. She strode along the path, even in her anger appreciating the sun setting over the sea, which turned the sand and rocks a deep gold. As the dew fell, it enhanced the smell of the vegetation lining the path, decorated with campion, bit-scabious and yarrow. On the other side of the barbed-wire fence, cows were munching, their lower jaws moving placidly from side to side as they ground up the grass torn up from the field. Gradually, she calmed down. Just as she reached the hotel beach, her mobile rang, startling in the evening's stillness.

'Hello?' Claire's voice was wary.

'Claire? Are you all right?' Emily sounded concerned.

'Emily...' Claire acknowledged. 'Yes, I'm fine, thanks. Nothing a good walk hasn't sorted. Given me thinking time. Did you bump into Daniel? He saw me, and I thought he was going to come over and talk, but then the barriers went up and he turned away. It made me realise you were right, and I can't take this any further than friendship. In fact, I'm not sure even friendship is an option at the minute,' she finished grimly.

'I'm sorry. Yes, we had a chat with him and offered him a lift back. We've just dropped him off at the hotel. He told us he'd had a guest yesterday, which I assume was that woman, right? Then it was weird because he was very insistent we should tell you he'd taken her to the station this morning, and she'd appreciated the small bedroom. He changed the subject after that, but I suppose you understand what he was saying? Sounds like whatever she was there for never happened.'

Claire stood, frozen in place.

Damn the man! Just as she'd conceded defeat, he turned round and sent her a message like that. Oh, yes, she understood what he meant, but if he'd wanted her to know he'd not slept with that woman, why hadn't he simply come over when they were in the pub, and told her himself?

'Anyway, you're sure you're okay?'

'I'll live, and thanks.'

The evening had darkened. An occasional gull made a half-hearted cry, and the white foam tops of the wave glistened against the shadowed sea. Stars scattered themselves over the velvet dimness of the sky, and a lighter glow to the west was all that remained of sunset.

Claire stared thoughtfully at the cottage, half way along the beach, which showed no lights. If Jake and Emily had given him a lift back to the hotel, it was likely he was back, and by the look of things, had gone to bed. Good, because she really didn't feel like coping with Daniel Morgan this evening. With luck, she'd get past, even though the current state of the tide didn't allow for her to walk out very far. Dropping onto the beach, she made her way along the sands, and when she reached the cottage, she held her breath, silently moving past.

A figure rose from one of the patio chairs and stepped forwards. 'Claire? Is that you?'

'Daniel!' Shock exploded throughout her whole body, and her heart raced. Hell! 'What do you want?'

'To talk.' He advanced to the wall, a dark figure against the white walls of the cottage. 'Just to talk, Claire. Come here. Please?'

Claire looked at him. She couldn't move, and she couldn't stop her next barbed comment. 'Where's your *girlfriend*?'

'I took her to the station this morning and asked Emily to let you know I'd sent her home. And… last night? She slept in the spare room. You need to know that.' He came slowly to the gate and opened it. 'Claire?'

Reluctantly, she climbed the short flight of steps and went onto the patio. They stood facing each other, oblivious to the fading daylight, the gentle sound of waves, an occasional bird call. He reached out to touch her, gently, on the cheek. Her skin shivered at his touch, and his hand slid down her cheek to lie warm and heavy against her neck before he dropped it to his side. He leaned forward, his face ghostly in the dim light. She could smell whisky on his breath.

'You've been drinking!' She turned away, arms crossed defensively round her body.

'Oh, yes,' he said softly. 'But I'm not drunk, Claire. A pint of beer and two whiskies don't make you drunk, although they might take the edge off your will-power, your determination to withstand temptation. If I was sober I'd not be here, waiting for you, and if I was drunk, I'd not be here either, so there you are.' He straightened up and reached towards her again, cupping her face before letting his hands slide down to lie on her shoulders. 'I want to talk to you, that's all.'

Claire swallowed, the breath leaving her body, her stomach lurching, her legs turning weak. She dug her nails into the palms of her hands and prayed the thudding of her heart wasn't audible, for it would surely give away how he affected her.

What was he going to talk about? Would he finally tell her what had upset him so much and made it impossible for him to trust, to *love*, another woman?

CHAPTER 15

'I ONLY WANT TO TALK,' he repeated, shaking his head, removing his hands, and stepping back. Anguish filled his voice. 'You need to know why I'm like this, why I'm so frightened to let myself love you, even though I want to. It started with my mother. She only wanted to socialise, and she was a self-centred woman. Not interested in her husband or me.'

Daniel half-turned away from Claire. He felt shame and anger, but this time, he was determined to explain. 'My wife—my *ex*-wife—completed what my mother began, and finished me. I lost my self-respect... my ability to trust and to love, too. It took Gina a few years, several lovers and quite a few cruel taunts, and it was slow and very painful. A couple of weeks ago, she came back to our house—*my* house. I was an idiot. I'd not changed the locks, you see. She came with yet another of her lovers, and she was pregnant. It was impossible for me to stay because of what she'd done to me. Which is why I came here.'

His eyes dropped, and he rubbed his hands over his face. 'I'd been getting over her. Re-finding myself, I suppose. But her turning up like that, so callous, so fucking *arrogant* in the way she expected me to just roll over and let her stay—she sent me over the edge again. And there's more, but I can't—I *still* can't—bring myself to tell you the full extent of what she did. There was a baby…'

He heard the sharp intake of her breath, saw the unshed tears in her eyes, felt the gentleness of her touch as she laid her hand on his arm.

'Daniel, how terrible for you,' she murmured, her voice full of anguished tenderness.

There it was again—her complete understanding, her sympathy, her compassion. No recriminations about Louise. He wasn't ready to form a new relationship, but she undermined all his vows to keep away from her. He didn't think he could take any more, and yet… what if?

Those two brief words were like a beam of light in the darkness that filled his mind.

What if?

He continued his explanation. 'Then I met you. So lovely. So honest. So brave. But don't you see? I've lost all my confidence. I don't feel as if I can ever trust another woman again. *That's* what they've done, between them. I'd nearly sorted myself out, but she returned, and brought it all back. All those stupid feelings of not being worthy. I need to find myself again and then maybe… maybe…' He closed his eyes and breathed deeply, fists clenched by his side. Logically, he knew there were kinder women in the world than his mother and his ex-wife, but his faith had been shaken too many times.

After their divorce, and because of what had happened with the baby, he'd been in such a mess he'd gone to a counsellor. The man had clarified everything for him. Gina was a similar type to his mother, and he'd subconsciously been looking for love and approval from her and missed the warning signs. Because of his experiences as a child, and with Gina, yes, he had trust issues, maybe even difficulty in expressing his love. The man had helped him enormously, had told him he'd heal and to give himself time and avoid any sort of deep relationship until he felt he'd regained his equilibrium. He'd warned him it would be gradual, and not to force things.

'You have to know this—I've been under the care of a counsellor for six months. He told me to give myself time to heal.'

He stood with his head bowed, wondering what her response would be to his confession of being unable to manage his feelings alone.

Her hands slid up his arms and round the back of his neck as she tugged him gently towards her.

His eyes flew open.

That was her response?

He came towards her as if walking through water, his gaze fixed on hers.

Claire pulled his head down, and all he could see was tenderness and sorrow filling her face. Unable to help himself, an explosion of relief bursting through him, as his mouth accepted her kiss of compassion and comfort.

And he was the one who changed it.

His lips were soft and warm as they searched, learning the taste, the shape, of her mouth. His tongue sought entry and caressed hers with slow intimacy. The only other contact between them was her hands, the feel of her warm fingers on his nape.

He drew back and looked questioningly into her eyes before moving into another slow, sensuous kiss that filled him, sang to him, dazzled him, as he lifted his hands to smooth them along her jaw, her cheeks, finally settling on her shoulders, gentle as a butterfly's touch.

Now he was kissing her, he thrust the firmly avowed intention *just to talk* to the back of his mind. It was impossible to draw back, impossible to stop the storm engulfing him. Inside, he was humming with joy and desire. He felt anxiety as well, but for now, his apprehension was over-ridden by the sensuousness of his feelings, the rising heat of his body, an overwhelming desire to give, to pleasure her... *worship* her.

He needed her sweetness, her gentleness, her kindness, her *love*! They'd already started to heal him, for otherwise he would never have poured out his shame and bitterness. They could talk tomorrow... and tomorrow, as they said, was another day. At the moment, there was only Claire...

She was responding to him freely—responding to the passion he was creating simply with his lips and tongue. She trembled and arched her head back as his mouth trailed over her throat and his head lowered to her breasts, his breath warm on the skin at the opening of her shirt.

'Take it off?' he beseeched.

He saw her hands shaking as she reached for the buttons, fumbling with the simple action needed to release button from button-hole.

His hands took over. They slid from her shoulders, over her breasts, and closed over hers, pushing them gently out of the way. Their eyes remained locked as he slowly and deliberately undid button after button. When, finally, her shirt hung open, he swept it off her shoulders in one fluid movement before bending his dark head to the swell of her breasts, his hands impatient as they reached behind her to free the clasp of her bra.

Claire whimpered deep in her throat. She tried to reach for him but he gently lowered her hands back to her sides, all the while his mouth searching her body, kissing her, his lips tenderly teasing her as he caressed with knowing hands, featherlight on her back, her sides, dipping gently, sensuously, into the waistband of her jeans. Then he took her hand and led her inside and up the stairs to the bedroom.

'Daniel... Daniel, please...' Claire pleaded weakly, her hands sliding down his back as she pulled him nearer. Jeans and his shirt were abandoned. No problem now with an erection—his relief as she freed him was considerable. They sank onto the bed, his hands gentle on the satin of her thighs, continuing his delicate touches as she clung to his shoulders. He cupped her jaw in his hands, caressed her face with his lips, inhaling the uniqueness of her smell, her shampoo, all female, all the while murmuring, kissing, as he swept her along. His fingers slipped inside and found her hot, wet centre, caressing it until he felt her muscles tense, felt her hover and, finally, felt her arch against him, closing round his fingers, crying out his name. He was aware of the tremor of her aftershocks and held himself back for a few moments, an overwhelming awe sweeping through him, knowing *he* had caused this ecstasy, and she was so beautiful to see, as her orgasm overwhelmed her.

But a few moments were all before Daniel slid deep into her warmth, his hands still caressing, still causing Claire to writhe and beg, as his mouth sought her lips, her eyelids, her jaw, the delicate shell of her ear, as he whispered words of love.

He stilled, and raised his head, his eyes wide.

Finally, *finally*, he knew he'd come home.

His throat closed, and like a blazing fire, warmth exploded in his chest, as his eyes blurred with unshed tears of joy. In this moment, he worshipped her body, her spirit, her mind. He moved again, his thrusts starting with slow anticipatory pleasure before becoming deeper and more rapid until, with an inarticulate shout, he shuddered to a climax, laying claim to her body, his sheer exuberant bliss overwhelming him with ecstasy. Looking at her with eyes full of sunshine breaking through the grey, he touched his lips to hers, a gentle kiss of thanks, a tender offering made to the very centre of her being, before dropping his head to rest on her soft breasts. Claire's arms slid up to cradle his head, as they both lay sated and exhausted in the aftermath.

Time passed. Daniel stirred. Without speaking, he rolled onto his side and took Claire in his arms, gazing at her, knowing he had something to give after all. He could give her friendship, yes, they'd already proved that, but he could also give her love and pleasure. Revering her body, he kissed her, stroked his fingers over her breasts and let his hands tantalise every part of her. Her response was immediate as she clung to him, her fingers moving over him as surely as his moved over hers. His mouth caused more sweet chaos as he trailed his searching lips over her neck, then moved lower, to seek her breasts, before returning to take possession of her mouth with an intensity that caused every part of his body to weaken as his desire suffused him. The second climax was as fulfilling as the first and finally, exhausted, their bodies slicked with sweat, limbs tangled in languorous satisfaction, they slept.

It was in the cold light of early dawn, when Daniel awoke, and turned to look at the sleeping face on the pillow next to him, that the enormity of what had happened struck him, and panic set it.

Why had he done this?

Last night, he hadn't planned for it. He'd only intended to explain, with as little detail as possible, about his ex-wife. But Claire's sympathy had blazed from her eyes and then there had been that kiss.

That one, tender kiss.

He didn't think she'd intended it to be passionate—

more one of love and sympathy for his pain—but it'd been his undoing

And this morning, Daniel's apprehension returned in full force.

No-one could live with the self-doubts he would bring to a relationship, no matter how hard he tried not to. He had to go off to America soon, and he didn't think he'd be able to leave Claire without wondering what she was doing the whole time he was away. He'd be distracted by suspicion.

Daniel dropped his head into his hands, overwhelmed. *He wasn't ready*. His trust had been shattered into a million pieces and he'd not yet put it back together. Until he did, he was spoiled goods.

It would be better if he went now. He could take the memory of last night with him, fresh and whole in his mind. Claire would get over him in a few weeks.

But what if she didn't… what if she waited for him?

What if?

Was there hope for him?

Hope for *them* in some not-too-distant future?

Ah, yes, indeed… what if?

Slipping from the bed, Daniel hastily showered before finding his abandoned clothes and dressing, all the time berating himself. When Claire had kissed him so gently, he should have pulled back, seen it for what, initially, it was—a kiss of support and caring. He should have told her to go up to the hostel.

But now?

He had to go.

CHAPTER 16

It was late when Claire awoke. Stirring luxuriously, she remembered the shared passion of last night, the words that had been spoken at the height of their lovemaking, the feel of Daniel's hands on her body, and her response to him. A smile curved her mouth, and she stretched like a cat, reaching out a hand to find him. Her hand fell on the sheet. Startled, she rolled over, eyes snapping open to see the space next to her empty, only the dent in the pillow showing where Daniel had been.

Of course. Claire smiled at her panic. He would be in the shower, or downstairs, or perhaps had gone for an early morning walk.

The shower was empty but scattered drops told her Daniel had been there before her. Stepping in, she lifted her face to the warm spray. She couldn't keep the memory of their lovemaking out of her mind and Claire shivered with sensuous pleasure. A secret smile flitted across her face as heat pooled inside, wishing he was here, his mouth slick on her wet skin as his fingers worked their magic.

Running downstairs, Claire pushed open the door to the kitchen, joy putting a bounce in her step and a song on her lips. She hummed as she walked straight over to the kettle. There would be more nights with Daniel, days of getting to know him, years of sharing his life, and finally banning the distrustful look in his eyes, the wary set of his mouth.

Turning, she jerked back in shocked surprise.

He was there. Daniel was sitting at the table, an empty mug in front of him. His head was bowed, his body still.

Somehow, even without being able to see his expression, Claire could sense his despair. What was this? Eyeing him cautiously, she moved to sit on the chair next to him, stretching out her hand and gently laying it over his tense fingers.

'I thought you'd gone out, for a walk maybe?'

He continued to sit in stony silence, his fingers remaining rigid under hers.

'Daniel?'

'Nothing's changed,' he said, shifting restlessly, looking at her with sadness in his eyes. 'If I stayed, I'd poison us. You'd hate me in a month.'

Oh, how he infuriated her even as she loved him with all her heart. Why on earth was he being so stupid, especially now, after last night? There was so much they could share—painting, an interest in the gardens, their love of books, art and music. She loved his humour, his acute mind, the way they'd so quickly come to share joy in the simple things they'd done together in such a short time.

She loved his body, as well. The strength, the leanness, his hands, so long-fingered which last night had played her to a crescendo. Their lovemaking had been passionate, and each had cared for the needs of the other.

Yet… what about his trip to America? How would they get round that? She wasn't going to throw over this chance in a lifetime job and follow him. She *couldn't*. Had they built a strong enough relationship to withstand the separation? No, they hadn't. Not strong enough to last so long. Okay, there were ways round this. He couldn't come back during his ten months, but surely, she could take some holiday in the winter and fly over there?

'Why? Why would I hate you?' Her voice was an impassioned plea.

Daniel stood, strode over the back door, hesitated, then returned, dropping back into his seat, his fingers fidgeting with his cup, turning it round and round. 'Because I'm not sure I could trust you, and you'd be angry, and rightly so,' he answered with a bitter simplicity. 'Last night, I never intended to make love to you. I honestly only came to talk.' He swung sideways in the chair, his movements edgy, to stare out of the window. After a few moments, he turned back, his eyes sad. 'I don't want to hurt you. You're not the type to give something like that lightly, I know that...' He shook his head and buried his face in his hands, speaking with a muffled voice. 'I can only apologise for what happened, and say again, I never intended it.'

'It's something you may not want to hear, but I'm not sorry. I love you, flaws and all. I love you because I like who you are and we get on. I think we could make a go of things. I think we could sort this out.' Claire said imploringly, her heart in her voice. 'I accept I might have to live with your distrust for a while, but you'd soon realise I won't let you down.'

'Look, you know I've got to go to America. The whole time I'm there, I'm going to be wondering. Wondering if you'll become bored without me. Wondering if you'll take up with one of the group of people you're so friendly with down at the pub. Wondering if another guest will come along and charm you. I'll ask not-so-subtle questions, and you'll be hurt and upset and wonder what the future holds if I can't do something as essential as trust you in our relationship.'

'I think I could cope. We can have face-to-face talks. We can text and email. I could fly over in the winter.'

He hesitated. She saw it, saw the flash of hope briefly lighten his face before it closed down again.

'I *warned* you, remember? I told you to leave me be. Give me time, Claire. Give me time to sort myself out, okay? When I come back from America, I hope things will be better. I'd like to come back and we could try again? I'd like to, I really would.'

'What? A whole year apart and no communication between us? That's a hell of an ask, Daniel. We need to continue to build on what we've started here.'

He huffed out a breath and stood up. 'Okay. I'll leave you my details. We can stay in touch. But for now, I think really it might be best if I go. I'm mixed up and need time to think. I need time to be sure Gina's ghost isn't going to stalk our relationship. When she's banished, I hope you'll still be here, because I *will* come back.' His eyes pleaded with her. 'If you'll wait? If you'll give me that time?'

Claire sat as if frozen. She couldn't speak. Her throat had closed up. Whether from misery or fury, she wasn't too sure.

After a long silence, he swung round and in seconds had gone from the room.

A few moments later, she heard him go upstairs, only to return a few minutes later, followed by the slam of the door. Galvanised to her feet, she raced to the door and ran round the side of the cottage. There, she watched unbelievingly as Daniel strode to his car, parked at the bottom of the access road, with a case in his hand. He must have gone up for the car earlier. This was all planned. She was too stunned, too shocked to call out as he drove slowly away.

Returning to the cottage, she let the door close, and leaned back against it, her heart cold inside her. This was caused by more than Gina and her infidelity. Raking through her mind for what he'd told her, she remembered something. A baby, he'd said. And stuff he couldn't tell her. What on earth had he meant? What stuff? Was it something to do with the baby?

Moving to the table, she sat down, her head in her hands. She'd have to talk to him again, try to show him that whatever had happened before, this was different. Yet he'd taken his case…

Leaping to her feet she ran lightly upstairs and into the bedroom where only hours before he'd carried her to such dazzling orgasms.

She knew he'd arrived with very little, and it didn't take long to discover there wasn't a single possession of his left anywhere. He'd obviously been packing everything up as she'd slept. He must have been incredibly quiet while in the bedroom.

But on the bedside table was a slip of paper with an email address scrawled on it.

So he'd really meant it, that he was leaving sooner than intended. Claire didn't know what to think. He wanted her to sit here and wait for him? For a year? By which time, he'd indicated he would have sorted himself out. Well, *shit*! That was some request. Fury vied with sympathy. Hatred warred with love. A *whole fucking year*?

If she had an ounce of backbone, she'd head off to Solhaven, pull Paul into his office, and ravish him.

But that was a silly thought. She'd do no such thing because, as she'd already told Daniel, she wasn't like that. She wouldn't betray him with someone else, no matter how tentative things had been left between them.

Was she sure he'd left, though? Maybe the case was for something else? Maybe he had to go back to London for a few days? Emily would know if he'd gone for good because he would have checked out and paid.

Half an hour after Daniel had left, Claire dropped into a chair next to Emily's desk. 'Has Daniel been in this morning?'

Emily tilted her head. 'Yes. About half an hour ago, and he paid what was owing. Seemed in a hurry. What's happened, Claire? He never mentioned leaving last night.'

Head in hands, Claire told her everything, leaving Emily looking thoughtful as she came to the end, explaining Daniel wanted time to get properly sorted out, but had said he would come back. Where he'd gone until it was time for him to go to America in September, neither Claire nor Emily knew. Only the cold fact he'd settled up, left the keys and said his farewell.

Emily shook her head. 'I'm sorry, Claire, it's a very hard thing he's left you to cope with. Daniel is fragile, though, and I think he feels unable to move forward until he's sorted it. He's promised to come back, that's the only positive thing. If you're prepared to wait for a year?' Emily let her voice trail away, uncertainty lacing her words.

Claire finally let the tears she'd been holding back since he'd walked out of Gardener's Cottage that morning flow, until eventually, worn out, broken-hearted, she quietly slipped out of the hotel and went into the hostel to pack her things.

No need to stay there any longer. Not now.

Over the next few days every touch, every kiss, every word came back to haunt her. But as time passed, it became clear Daniel had meant what he'd said. He needed to get himself sorted out because he wanted to come to her without the emotional problems which had haunted him for so long, and so far, he'd not replied to any of her emails.

But not all of him had gone.

It didn't take Claire long to realise she had to eat properly again and take better care of herself. She knew there was something for her in the future after all, something cherished and precious, something she could cling to until Daniel, as she was sure he would, returned.

And eventually, she had to tell her family.

The opportunity arose on November the fifth. They'd all been down to Solhaven for the annual bonfire and fireworks and afterwards returning to Claire's for a bonfire supper.

When they'd all eaten, Claire looked from one to the other of them, and they, beginning to realise something was the matter, gradually stopped talking.

'I'm pregnant,' Claire blurted out.

They all spoke at once.

'When's it due?'

'Daniel Morgan?'

'Oh, Claire, cariad. It doesn't matter. We'll stand with you.'

Claire answered Emily first. 'About four months after yours, so April, sometime. I promise I'll get onto the ads for another gardener, now. Definitely going to need someone to cover my maternity leave, but the joy of this job is I can have the baby with me most of the time. And none of you have to say it—I know we were incredibly stupid about birth control, but it was one of those heat of the moment things which just overtook us.'

'We understand, sweetie. No worries. Not what we planned for, but it'll all work out. Sasha's coming down soon, and I'll be working from home. You could leave the little one with me if it was cold, or raining, or you had to go somewhere to buy plants?'

'I could, and that's lovely of you. Let's see how things go, okay?'

Claire turned to Jake, her sentences jerky. 'Yes, of course Daniel. And neither of us meant this to happen, you must realise that. He told me he'd come back, once his time in America was up, and he left me his email address. I've sent a few messages—just easy, chatty ones—and he's not replied. I don't know what to do, because I honestly thought we'd keep in touch while he's away. I don't want to push things again.'

Her mum had been rubbing her back while she was talking to Jake and Emily, and now Claire gave her a grateful smile. 'Another grandchild, mum. Bet you didn't expect that!'

Annie looked pleased. 'How wonderful—two cousins who can grow up together! Two candidates for surfing lessons, eh, Jake?' Annie patted her son's hand. 'Jake? Jake! You're miles away.'

'What? Oh, yeah, sorry, mum. I was thinking about Daniel. A very sad guy, but you have to feel sorry for him.'

Claire looked tired. 'Come on, Jake. I know he had problems with his ex, and they lost their baby, but to leave me as he did, leaving everything so up in the air, and what's even worse, not keeping in touch? I'm not sure I feel very forgiving at the moment.'

'Don't be too hard on him.'

'Look, I'm sad his mother was uncaring and his wife was into having lovers, but he said he loved me and he'd —oh, *hell!*' Claire wiped a tear from her cheek as her sadness over Daniel's desertion hit her again. She thought she'd got it under control. She caught hold of her mum's hand, needing comfort.

Jake looked uncertain. 'He didn't tell you the real reason she fucked him up, then?'

'Other than having affairs and the and turning up at his house, pregnant with yet another lover in tow? And they lost a baby. Wasn't that enough?'

'Well, he's gone now, and I don't know when we'll see him again, so I see no harm in telling you. Might make you understand him better.' Jake fell silent for a few minutes, staring at his clasped hands lying on the table, then huffed out his breath, sitting back in his chair, and looking at each of them in turn. 'Daniel always wanted children. Really wanted them.'

Claire's hand went to the slight bump under the loose-fitting sweater she wore and remembered his face when he'd held the little baby back in the summer, outside the café.

'When they first married, his wife was all sweetness and light. He told me there'd been a couple of short-lived affairs, and when he'd found out, she threw herself at him, weeping and begging for a fresh start. As far as Daniel knew, she kept her word for a few months, during which she told him she was pregnant.'

Claire's heart ached for him. He'd said he'd never had the chance to know his baby. But an unfaithful wife, a miscarriage—these were things people got over. She'd tried to show him support and friendship, had damped down her physical attraction, but it hadn't been enough. Maybe he'd been right when he said he needed to get away and sort himself out. When he came back, she hoped everything in his life would be right for him, she really did. Then maybe they could try again. But she still felt an edge of anger to all her thoughts, especially because he'd not answered her emails. He'd claimed to be confused and mixed up, but by hell, so was she, now. She hung onto his promise he'd be back, even while wondering if he'd meant it. He'd talked of her maybe finding someone else while he was away, but the reverse also applied, and the possibility existed as a small nugget of fear lodged in her chest.

Jake started talking again, breaking into her reverie. 'He went with her for a scan, when she was fourteen weeks pregnant. Although not one hundred percent certain, the hospital thought she was having a girl. They said they could confirm it at eighteen-weeks.'

Claire wondered if it had been a miscarriage or had happened after the baby had been born. Leaning forward, she kept her eyes intently on her brother.

'He was over the moon. Then she met another man

because, she told Daniel, it bored her to stay at home. He asked her the date of the eighteen-week scan and told her he'd still be coming with her. She laughed in his face. Apparently, she'd been away for a couple of days, and told him she'd used his money to stay in a private clinic and have a termination. The baby didn't fit into her scheme of things, especially his baby.'

'Wha-a-t? She did *what?*' Claire had jumped to her feet, her fists clenched, eyes wide, her heart filled with cold horror.

'Deliberately ended her pregnancy. Daniel found the strength to throw her out and sue for divorce, but then he had a bit of a break-down. Hardly surprising, really.' Jake's mouth turned down at the corners, his eyes sombre. 'He told me he'd been with a counsellor for a few months, with depression and self-esteem issues, and just when he thought he'd come to terms with it all, she turned up with another lover, obviously pregnant, and told him she was going to keep this one because her boyfriend's parents were stinking rich and wanted a grandchild. That's when he came down here, after Sebastian Whitchurch told him about Solhaven. It was to escape her.'

Claire's hands flew up, and she covered her mouth, tears in her eyes. 'Oh, shit. And I stuck my nose in and pushed at him and tore the poor bloke in half. Oh, *shit*! How could she do that? She's a monster! I wish… I wish I hadn't tried telling him everything was okay and he could trust me. I wish I hadn't thrown myself at him. It really wasn't all right, was it?' Her remorse was deep and tears escaped to run down her cheeks. Trying to imagine what he'd felt like when his ex-wife had told him, was too much. She simply couldn't bear it.

Emily looked thoughtful, her hands protectively covering her now-considerable baby bump. 'That's harsh. But from what you're saying, he's been more affected by the loss of his baby than by Gina's affairs?'

'I think so, yes.' Jake looked pensive. 'I got the impression her behaviour had stopped having an effect by then, and he'd given up on all hope of a relationship, but what she did with his baby broke him.'

'This is going to sound strange,' Emily looked round at them all. 'Might it be better, for Claire, if she *doesn't* tell him about the baby? No, wait, hear me out.' She held up her hand against the torrent of voices from all sides. 'If he comes back in the summer, we know he's got himself straight and has come back specifically for Claire's sake. The baby will be icing on the cake. If we tell him about the baby, and he rushes back, it leaves Claire in a similar position to the one he's in—can she trust his love for her, or did he just want his child? Claire has a strong support network. Emotionally it might be better if Daniel was on the scene, but I'd like to see him come back for just one reason, and that's for you, sweetie.' She held out her hand and clasped Claire's, smiling at her tenderly. 'And if he doesn't come back, then yes, you'll have to tell him. It's only fair. I guess we'll know by the end of August?'

Claire waved as they all finally left, feeling grateful and exhausted, with sombre thoughts drifting through her mind. If Daniel decided never to come back, it would break her heart, but he had a right to know about the baby. They'd have to come to some sort of arrangement, because there was no way she would keep his child from him, so yeah, go along with what Emily had suggested, and by the end of August, she'd know.

If he hadn't shown, she'd have to tell him.

CHAPTER 17

DANIEL'S last lecture had been delivered, his last talk given. Now the end of June, and he was supposed to spend the next two months at a summer school up in Alaska, with an entire group of American seascape and landscape artists. He didn't want to go and had sent his excuses. Personal matters at home which needed his attention. Completely true.

He wanted to go home. More especially, he wanted to go back to Solhaven. Ever since leaving, part of his mind had dwelt on Claire and how she must have felt when he abandoned her. It was a harsh thing, to leave her as he had, but he hoped she'd understood, and believed in him when he'd told her one day, he'd go back.

After ten months of intense work and, in-between, a lot of wandering along lonely coastlines, he felt healed and secure in himself, and also at peace.

He'd put Gina and his mother in the past. None of it was his fault.

He was also accepting of the fact his baby daughter still nestled in his heart and always would.

He was more than ready to go back, heart-whole and healed.

He'd ignored Claire's messages, and eventually they'd stopped. He thought it was better that way. Twice, feeling homesick, wanting to be with her, he'd sent emails to her. Brief communications, saying little other than he hoped she was well, and he still intended to return. Her response had simply been a thumbs up emoji, which had left him feeling... disappointed. But what could he expect, after his initial, pointed silence? Since then, he'd concentrated on his work engagements and solitary ramblings.

Now, he needed to see her in person.

He *had* to see her.

He was going back to Solhaven, to find out if he and Claire had survived. He hoped she would still be there, working on her wonderful restoration, and would forgive—no, *had* forgiven—his absence. He hardly dared to consider she might have found someone else, but if she had, he hoped he'd be strong enough to leave her in peace.

It was a resolve he really didn't want to put to the test.

Several days later, Daniel's chin dark with the close-cropped beard he'd grown while in America, he pulled into the Haven House Hotel's car park. The solidly grey Victorian mansion was indeed a haven. He'd subconsciously recognised that last year, but with the conflict in his mind, he'd not been able to fully appreciate the peacefulness of the house, with its sweeping views down to the low cliffs and the glittering sea. He could just see the roof of Gardener's Cottage, and judging by the appearance of the gardens, Claire was continuing to do a magnificent job. Sitting in his car, his trembling hands resting on the wheel, apprehension filled him and his whole body shook as he considered his utter arrogance. His absence from this place, his absence from her, with hardly any communication, must have hurt her, and now he was returning, hoping she would've waited for him, and accept his presence back in her life. His previous calm certainty had deserted him. It took him nearly ten minutes before he dared to step out of the car.

Entering the hall, which he remembered had been cleverly turned into a reception area, there was no sign of Emily. Another lady, tall and dark-skinned, stood behind the desk. She was very striking, and Daniel immediately wondered if he could get her into one of his pictures.

'Sir.' She smiled at him, a dimple creasing her cheek.

'Hi. Do you have any rooms free?' Her name tag said Sasha Fielding. He placed his hands on the antique desk to stop their trembling.

Turning her attention to a slim laptop on the desk, she tapped a few keys. 'We've four rooms. They vary in size and price. We've a suite, with a bedroom and small sitting-room, and a balcony which looks out to the coast, which is our most expensive, but very delightful, room…' She paused and raised an eyebrow in his direction.

'I'll take it. And the Bradstocks? I was hoping to see them. I assume they're still here?' He was confident, with the commitment Jake had to the café and Emily's plans for the hotel, they'd be around somewhere, and it would be good if he could sound them out. 'I was here for a few weeks last year, and I got to know them well.'

'Ah. Yes, they're here. Shall I ring through and let them know you're asking for them, Mr—er, Mr?'

'Morgan. Daniel Morgan. Yes, please do.' Daniel was fully aware of a slight flash of surprise crossing her face. So Sasha Fielding knew his name. Perhaps she was more than just an employee, then?

Handing over his card, receiving a key card in return, Daniel wandered over to the window at one side of the front door, and looked out over the gravelled drive and parking area. The gardens were flourishing now, and the manicured flower beds surrounding the house looked beautiful in the summer sun. It was nearly a year since he'd left and Claire had obviously worked hard.

He froze as someone pushing a wheelbarrow came into view from his left, and his heart thumped, palms growing damp with nervousness.

Claire!

But no, *not* Claire, he realised almost immediately, as the figure rounded the corner. Too tall, too broad, and dark-haired. A man. Did that mean Claire was no longer here? Had she left because of him? He must have hurt her by leaving, but it had still been the best thing to do, it really had. Returning now a much stronger man, Daniel knew there was hope for them… *if* she was still here, and *if* she'd still accept him. He felt sick at the thought he might have driven her away from the place and the job she loved so much, when for the entire time he'd been gone, he'd visualised her here, taking comfort from imagining her at work.

'Daniel.'

That was Jake's voice. Swinging round, Daniel smiled tentatively. He was uncertain of his welcome. After all, he'd messed Claire around, and as her brother, Jake might feel pissed about it. But the surfer was smiling, a hand outstretched. Stepping forwards, Daniel shook it, even more reassured when Jake slapped his shoulder.

'Come and have a coffee in the lounge. Are you just calling round, or staying?'

'I've booked a room. How's Emily?' His words rushed out, the two sentences jostling each other. He hardly dared mention Claire.

'Nursing Olivia at the moment. She'll bring her down and join us as soon as she's done.'

A flash of pain hit Daniel. He suspected it would be there every time someone mentioned babies, but it was an acceptable pain now. 'Congratulations!' His smile of delight was genuine. 'How old is she?'

'She was born in January, so six months. They develop so quickly. She can sit up and loves being played with—' Jake stopped abruptly, probably remembering the sorry tale Daniel had told him, the first day he was in the cottage.

'It's okay, Jake,' Daniel murmured. 'I've come a long way since last year. That's why I've come back.'

They sat down in a corner of the large sitting-room, near one of the French windows. A server came across and Jake asked for coffees, checking with Daniel first as to preference.

'Okay, you've come a long way, you said. So, how's things, because I'm assuming you mean mentally, as well as physically?' Jake's smile was in place as always, but now they were sitting down, Daniel saw his eyes were the icy blue of a winter's sky, and knew he was being questioned because of Claire, rather than Jake being chatty.

'Yes. And it's good. If it hadn't been for Gina tipping me over the edge again, I would've been fine last year. My counsellor said a year ago I was nearing the end of the grieving phase, but Gina set me off again. I might have been okay, even then, but...' his voice trailed off.

'Claire pushed you a bit, didn't she?'

'A bit,' Daniel admitted, ruefully. 'But I had feelings for her, too, and she sensed that.'

'Had?'

'*Have*. Oh, yes, I have feelings for her. But I don't know about her, now, do I? I may have totally pissed her off, and she's simply wiped me from her mind and moved on? Although I told her I'd come back.' His hand trembled as he picked up his coffee, and misgiving quivered through him. 'I've finally put everything behind me.'

Jake nodded. 'It's all good, then, isn't it?'

'It is, as long as Claire's still around and willing to see me again.'

'Why wouldn't she be round?' Jake looked surprised.

'I saw a gardener while I was waiting for you, and it's a bloke?'

'Ah, yes. The mysterious Anton.'

Daniel cocked an eyebrow and leaned back, crossing one leg over the other. 'Mysterious?'

'Very mysterious,' Jake nodded. 'Claire took him on about four months ago. She'd always intended to have another gardener, but it kept getting postponed for various reasons. Then it, um, became rather imperative. There weren't many applicants, and out of the ones who applied, she took on Anton. He seems to have a natural gift for gardening, but he won't say anything about where he comes from, or whether he has family. Friendly enough and gets on well with Claire. Don't glower, Daniel. Gets on well doesn't mean interested, okay?'

Daniel's eyebrows lifted as he gave a short laugh. 'Was it so obvious?'

'Your glower? Yeah.' Jake leaned forward, forearms resting on his thighs.

Daniel still had the canvas he'd started of Jake surfing, and he hoped to go back to his people and sea theme. The long-planned exhibition for this autumn would use paintings from his loft, which he'd done over the years, and which he'd hastily cobbled together since his return from America. Safe ones. Seascapes only, but no people. While away, many of his works had been dark and stormy, purely elemental. Once they arrived from America, maybe some could be used for this exhibition, maybe not. Daniel didn't care too much. Painting them had helped to re-balance his emotions.

'Is Claire still living in Gardener's Cottage?'

'Yeah, she is.'

A silence fell, but for Daniel, he didn't feel it was an easy one, despite Jake's apparent friendliness. He felt he was having to dig for information about Claire out of her brother. Jake was volunteering nothing. He rubbed a hand over his chin, still surprised to feel the soft, dense growth on his face. He could easily shave it off, and liked to keep it clipped pretty short, anyway, but if Claire—his thoughts stumbled to a halt.

'Is she at home now?' Daniel abruptly stood. 'I think the best thing for me to do is go down there myself and face her. I don't want you brokering a meeting. If I go down, I'll see how she reacts and if she's not prepared, I suspect I'll hear more truth than platitudes.'

'Good thinking, mate. Yeah, she's at home.'

Daniel stared at Jake, his brow creasing. There really was something he couldn't quite put his finger on. 'Okay. I'll see you later.'

'Do you want to borrow a buggy?'

'No, I'm good, thanks. I'll walk.'

'Good luck.' Jake looked serious. 'She's been waiting for you, you know. She's always been certain you'd come back.'

The two men exchanged a look.

'I'm sorry it took me so long,' Daniel finally said.

As he walked down the familiar path towards the small cottage he'd lived in for a month or two, Daniel's mouth went dry. In a few moments he'd come face to face with Claire and know, once and for all, if she'd forgiven him.

At least he knew she'd waited.

Jake's voice rang in his ears—*she's always been certain you'd come back.*

CHAPTER 18

'CLAIRE?'

Gasping, Claire, who'd been staring out across the beach, whirled round. Daniel stood there, just as she'd seen him so many times in her imagination. The same lean figure moulded by what seemed to be the same jeans. The white shirt, so fine she could see the shadow of his broad shoulders and chest through the material. His jaw—now, that was different because it was etched with a closely cropped beard, but it suited him. Oh, my, how it suited him.

Gone was his air of self-contained wariness, leaving a calmly resolute look on his face, an aura of confidence surrounding him, although… on closer inspection she detected fear in his eyes, and he was biting his lower lip.

Where had he sprung from? *Where on earth had he sprung from?*

Seeing him in front of her, she tried to speak, her mouth hanging inelegantly open. Colour flooded her face and her heart pounded. The same feelings she'd always felt on seeing Daniel swept through her: warmth, compassion, love, liking. Nothing—*nothing*—had changed about the way she felt.

Claire closed her mouth and lifted a trembling hand to brush her hair back from her face. Surely if he'd come back, it was because he felt better? She sank into a chair, uncertain whether she even wanted to hear what he had to say, in case it shot her hopes down in flames. Maybe, somehow, he'd heard about her pregnancy and had come seeking his child? After what had happened to him before, she could understand that.

'Daniel,' Claire replied faintly. Then, in a stronger voice, '*Daniel*!'

'May I sit?' He gestured to the other chair, his voice humble.

'Of course. Coffee? Tea? I can easily make—' She was babbling.

His raised hand cut her off. 'I just had a coffee at the hotel with Jake.'

Her thoughts whirled. Did he know? He must know. Why had he come back? He looked changed. He looked better. He sounded like the friend she remembered spending some happy times with, and not the unhappy man who'd been afraid to love her.

'Okay.' She gulped. She had to ask. She had to know whether he was here for her or just for the baby. If it was the baby... well, as she'd already decided, it would be understandable, but it would hurt. 'Okay, so why are you here? I got a couple of emails sometime last Christmas, saying you were all right, and you still wanted to come back one day. And now you just turn up?'

The way he looked at her then caused her stomach to turn a somersault and a horde of butterflies to release themselves inside. Her breathing quickened and her hands clenched on her lap, her fingernails biting into her palms.

He'd come back for her. There was no doubt, not from that look.

'Claire. Do you know I love saying your name? Do you know how many times I've said it to myself over the past year, as a promise to myself that if—no, *when*—I recovered, I'd come back, and say it to your face, along with a lot more? I didn't know what else to write after the emails I sent, and your response was… basic. I wondered if you wanted me to get out of your life, to be honest. Remnants of my lack of confidence, I guess.' His eyes were intent, his voice apologetic.

'You deserved that response. You'd ignored my earlier emails,' Claire said flatly.

'They were too soon after I'd left. I needed time to think.'

'Go on.'

'When I left you, it was the right thing to do, even though I know I hurt you. Making love that night wasn't on my agenda and it precipitated my decision to go, which made the whole thing worse for both of us.'

'No. Wait. There's something I need to say.' Because if she did, it would help him, she knew it would. 'I didn't completely understand what Gina had done. We'd been friends, and I loved that, but I wanted more and you

LOVE BY MOONLIGHT | 203

could sense it, which is why you felt under pressure. I pushed for that, and—'

He held up his hand to stop her. 'You didn't know the entire story, and you weren't to blame. I had to sort myself out. I couldn't cope with you on top of the dregs of Gina and her actions. Also, I need to tell you one last thing about Gina. About what she did. She—'

It was Claire's turn to interrupt. 'I know. Jake told me,' she said softly. 'He told me what she'd done to you.' Even now, especially now, her heart ached for the pain he must have suffered. 'Don't re-live it.'

Daniel bowed his head for a moment, then looked up. 'Okay. Okay. Anyway, I went to America after a few sessions with my counsellor, and took his advice to heart. I made sure I had plenty of time to myself, although the schedule they'd set up for me was manic. Even so, I managed a lot of time in wild places, so I could think. I never forgot you.' He smiled and reached out a hand, letting it lie on the table between them.

Slowly, Claire brought her hand from her lap and placed it in his. She felt a tingle from his warm fingers race up her arm and lodge in her heart, causing a starburst of joy.

'Claire, can we start over? Can I stay locally and come and see you, go for walks with you, take you out to dinner, continue with our friendship? I said I'd never forgotten you, but what I've not said is I left here with a small nugget of love and hope deeply buried inside, and it's grown to overwhelm me. You were my lodestone, and there were two words I carried with me as well—*what if?* What if I learned to love again, and you were there? Can we start over? Please, my darling?'

Tears filled her eyes, even as a soft warmth spread through her, together with a deep longing to hold him. 'Yes.'

'Just like that? No questions? No recriminations for running away?'

'I've already understood I didn't help matters. I didn't understand how wounded you were. Yes, I was upset you left. Of course I was. I was also upset it was for such a long time and you didn't want to communicate very much. But I accepted it was something you had to do. Let's put it behind us, all of it. Let's move into the future. And... I've a gift for you. I hope it's a gift you like and want, but I'm fairly optimistic you will.'

Claire stood and moved round the table, placing her hands on each side of his face as she leaned down and softly kissed him. His beard felt feathery beneath her fingers, and soft prickles from his moustache pressed into her lips.

He returned her kiss with equal gentleness, but it was enough to cause a heated longing to pool inside, as she remembered their love-making a year ago, and how he'd brought her to a couple of stunning climaxes during that passionate night. Pulling back, placing her hands on his shoulders, her breathing ragged, she murmured, 'Oh, Daniel, Daniel. I love you.'

Quite what would have happened next, she wasn't sure, but a wry grin crossed her face as she heard some small squeaks and whimpers.

Daniel's head tilted to one side, a look of puzzlement in his eyes.

Before he could quite work out what was making the noise, Claire swept up the small baby monitor from the window sill, concealing it down by her side.

'Stay there,' she said. 'Wait. I'll show you in a few moments.'

Flying up the stairs as if there were wings on her feet, she found Jamie just waking up. Gently gathering him up in her arms, she snuffled into his neck as he waved his hands and tried to catch hold of her hair.

'Shhh. Shush, sweet pea. Come. Come and meet your daddy.'

Carefully descending, Claire could see out of the front door that Daniel had stood, turned his back to the cottage and was looking at the sea, eternally advancing and retreating. She stepped onto the patio, feeling slightly apprehensive. What if this upset him too much? Oh, surely not. Surely not.

'Daniel,' she murmured, 'Daniel, come meet your son Jamie.'

Slowly, Daniel turned and looked from her to the baby in her arms, then back at her. His eyes widened and his face went white. 'My-my *son?*'

Claire nodded and took the few remaining steps to reach him. 'Here,' she whispered, holding Jamie a little way from her body. 'Hold him. Hold Jamie.'

Abruptly, Daniel went past her and Claire's heart plummeted. She'd done it again. She'd brought Jamie into things far too quickly.

But what else was she supposed to have done? Jamie

had been waking up. Full-blown crying would have soon followed. If she'd known Daniel was coming, she could have arranged for Jamie to go to Emily for the afternoon. She really ought to—

'Claire?'

She swivelled round, relief making her knees weak. Daniel had sat down and was now holding out his arms.

'I had to sit down,' he explained, his voice trembling. 'It's—I'm so shocked and I-I was worried I'd drop him.'

Claire could see a tremor in his hands as she gently stepped forwards and laid the baby in his arms. 'You can feed him. I express milk and keep a couple of bottles in the fridge. He comes with me to the gardens and it's easier to bottle feed him, especially with Anton flitting around.' Her mouth twitched in a smile as she laid the baby into Daniel's arms and disappeared to warm the bottle.

As she waited, a few tears ran down her cheeks. Tears of happiness and relief. Her heart was full.

Returning to the patio, Claire stopped. Daniel was gazing at his son with absolute wonder on his face, gently touching his cheek with one finger while firmly cradling him in his other arm.

'Little Jamie,' she heard him say. 'Little Jamie.' His voice broke as he bent his head and nuzzled his son's downy scalp.

Moving to stand beside him, he looked up at her, his eyes wet. 'So he didn't impede your lifestyle? And even though the father had run off, you were still steadfast and had him?'

'Yes. But I had a wonderful family to support me.

Having Jamie doesn't make me a saint. It's just my circumstances were good.'

He gave a small grimace. 'Gina had me.'

'She was wrong to do what she did. I don't think we need to say anything else on that subject.'

'Right as always. Here, give me his bottle. No doubt I'll make a complete hash of it and he'll never forgive me, but I've got to start somewhere!'

After Daniel had fed Jamie, and both of them had bathed him, they tucked him into his cot. The entire time, Daniel kept looking from her to Jamie as if he couldn't believe it. His eyes shone, his mouth was fixed in a permanent smile, and on one occasion, Claire was certain he swiped a tear from his cheek.

Once Jamie was asleep, they moved into the main bedroom, curling up on the bed, Daniel's arm round her shoulder as she leaned into his hard body.

Claire looked at him worriedly. 'I was going to email you, to let you know about Jamie. I thought it might help you after Jake told us about what Gina had done. But we had a family gathering and someone suggested if you knew about Jamie and came rushing back, I could never be certain you'd got over Gina and really loved me.'

Daniel paused and stared into space, his hand absently stroking her hair. 'I'm deeply sorry you went through your pregnancy alone, but whoever gave that advice was maybe wise. I'm glad I didn't know. Does that sound weird? If you'd told me before Christmas, yes, I would've come back. Of course I would, after what happened to my baby. But for me, that might have been too soon and my reasons might have been confused. It would also have been another emotional burden, although it sounds dreadful to call Jamie that.'

'You needed to work your way through everything, darling. No need to say sorry. I'm just glad you're not angry with me. I was going to tell you about Jamie whatever happened. I'd no right to keep him from you, so if you'd decided against returning, I was going to tell you.'

'How come you're so lovely?' Daniel murmured into her ear, while dropping kisses on her jaw and neck, his hand gently exploring her fuller breasts as she curled closer. Oh, the joy of being with him again was overwhelming, and her throat closed with emotion, holding him so tightly he protested he couldn't breathe.

His mouth covered hers, and they deepened their kiss, desire exploding after ten months apart. She yanked his shirt from the waistband of his jeans and took sheer pleasure in running her hands over his body, placing her mouth over each nipple and licking the hard nubs, letting her hand drift down to where he was hard, sliding down the zip and slipping her hand under the waistband of his boxers to touch the hot tip of his erection. When his fingers found her and he worked them into her wet centre, she convulsed round them, pushing her breasts against him and undulating her hips, a slave to his every touch.

There was no finesse, no patience, other than to grab a condom. They took off their clothes at speed, and rolled naked onto the bed, mouths seeking, teeth nipping, hands caressing.

She was so ready for him. Her wetness and warmth welcomed his hard perfection as she arched her body and pressed against him, begging, pleading, for release. He slipped his fingers between them, adding his touch to the other sensations to please her. The final cataclysmic explosion caused her body to tense and tighten round his him, making it impossible for him to hold back. She revelled in her power as he followed with his own release.

And a little later, a repeat performance, slightly slower, slightly gentler, just as passionate.

They lay curled round each other, warm and deeply content.

There was a lot to face in their future, but all of it good. Continuing their friendship, revelling in their lust, looking after Jamie—*together*.

Claire felt at peace.

Her belief in Daniel was justified, and their love would carry them through.

ACKNOWLEDGMENTS

No book is ever written without input, help and advice from numerous lovely people and the same applies here.

Special thanks to my editor Whitney Jones who continues helped me enormously and is still teaching me a lot – I shall forever be indebted to her for her kindness and hard work.

Thanks also to Romance Café Publishing for all their support and help in getting this series from its conception to its final form.

Thanks to my lovely beta readers Riana Everly, Jeanette Taylor Ford, Jude Srivalson, and MM Wakeford, who all managed to pick up on inconsistencies of various kinds and offered excellent constructive criticisms.

An especial mention must go to Riana Everly, for her help with my blurbs.

As always, thanks to my husband, for tolerating the time I spend writing, for making him listen while I work through an idea and for tolerating my mutterings when something isn't going right.

ALSO BY LIZ MARTINSON

Solhaven Forevers

Love By Sunset

Love By Moonlight

Love By Sunrise

Printed in Poland
by Amazon Fulfillment
Poland Sp. z o.o., Wrocław